He pu
shoul
him

Baby on the Run

KATE LITTLE

MILLS & BOON®

Pure reading pleasure™

First published in Great Britain 2009
by Harlequin Mills & Boon Limited,
Eton House, 18-24 Paradise Road, Richmond, Surrey TW9 1SR

ISBN: 978 0 263 87049 7

23-0609

Harlequin Mills & Boon policy is to use papers that are natural, renewable and recyclable products and made from wood grown in sustainable forests. The logging and manufacturing processes conform to the legal environmental regulations of the country of origin.

Printed and bound in Spain
by Litografia Rosés S.A., Barcelona

KATE LITTLE

claims to have lots of experience with romance – "the *fictional* kind, that is," she is quick to clarify. She has been both an author and an editor of romance fiction for over fifteen years. She believes that a good romance novel will make the reader experience all the tension, thrills and agony of falling madly, deeply and wildly in love. She enjoys watching the characters in her books go crazy for each other, but she hates to see the blissful couple disappear when it's time for them to live happily ever after.

In addition to writing romance novels, Kate also writes fiction and non-fiction for young adults. She lives on Long Island, New York, with her husband and daughter.

Chapter One

Carey Mooreland stared out at the highway, a frozen, four-lane blur, her gloved hands gripping the steering wheel so tightly her fingers ached. Snow that had begun falling a few hours earlier blew down even heavier now. Fat, white feathery flakes coated the windshield faster than the wipers could whisk them away.

The defroster on the old car wasn't working well and Carey reached up to wipe the foggy glass with her hand. It was the third car she'd owned in the past year, each model with more mileage and problems. But switching cars every few months had been another way to protect herself, to shield her identity and make it harder for Quinn to track her down as she moved from place to place.

She'd bought new snow tires in Vermont. An unexpected expense, but one she was glad of now. She had to think of her baby, Lindsay. The six-month-old little girl who slept snug in her car seat, covered from head to toe so that only her nose and a tiny portion of her sweet face showed as she slept.

Carey wanted to sleep, too. She wanted to turn around and go back to Blue Lake. She wanted to pull over and have a good cry. But like so many other times in the past year, she forced herself to do what she had needed to do to survive. To keep her baby safe. That was all that mattered to her now.

She switched on the radio, searching for some distraction from the rhythm of the squeaky wipers. A cheerful Christmas song filled the silence. It was Christmas Eve. She'd almost forgotten. Somehow during her desperate flight, the holiday—and all its glittering warmth—had faded into the dark cold night.

The highway had narrowed to one lane, thick with snow. She bumped along with few other cars in sight. She spotted a jack-knifed truck on the roadside, hazard lights blinking and she struggled to turn her eyes straight ahead again.

The small car swerved, despite the new tires. Carey finally gave up and decided to turn off. The car needed fuel and she needed some caffeine. She'd been concentrating so hard on her driving, she'd lost all track of direction. She knew she was somewhere on the coast of Maine. Somewhere between Blue Lake, Vermont, where she'd started, and Bar Harbor, where she hoped to board a ferry to New Brunswick, and from there, make her way to Prince Edward Island in Canada.

Canada was a big country. A person could hide there easily. After a while, even the obsessive Quinn McCauley would give up looking for her. That was her plan…and her prayer. If he was put behind bars, he'd be forced to give up. Or would he still have his underlings pursue her? She'd seen the way he held grudges. It wasn't out of the question.

She turned down the exit ramp and found herself at a stop sign on a dark road. A sign read, Greenbriar—5 miles. Gas. Food. Lodging. An arrow pointed to the right and Carey turned in that direction. It seemed the logical choice. She couldn't drive all night. Not in this storm. She needed to find a place to stay over and continue tomorrow morning. Hopefully the snowstorm would be over by then.

There might have been a few houses on the road, but Carey didn't see any. All she saw were tall trees and brush, covered with white. Not a single vehicle was in sight. It seemed everyone was staying in tonight. To celebrate. Or was just too wise to be out driving.

She and Lindsay would have been at a Christmas gathering right now, with her friends in Blue Lake—Rachel Reilly and her fiancé, Jack Sawyer, and their little boy, Charlie. Carey had left gifts for all of them and a note, explaining that she'd been suddenly called away to care for a sick relative, down in Virginia. She'd promised to get in touch in a few days.

She guessed they must have read her note by now. She tried to picture their reaction. She hated lying, especially to people who trusted her and helped her when she'd first arrived there. But she'd had no choice. She'd learned that Quinn's investigator had caught on to her trail again and if he traced her to Blue Lake, she didn't want her friends to point him in the right direction.

Someday I'll explain, Carey promised herself. Or maybe it was better not to. Better for everyone.

The Christmas song ended and the radio announcer started to report on Santa's flight, tracking his path from the North Pole around the entire world. Lindsay was too little know about Santa, but the sweet deception reminded Carey of the Christmas Eves of her past, when she was a little girl growing up happy and carefree. Feeling so safe and loved. Now her parents were both gone. And her husband, Tom, had died, too, in an accident last year on one of Quinn's construction sites.

She was all alone except for Lindsay. Her secret was like a wall around her heart, as thick as any prison, making it impossible to grow truly close to anyone, to make lasting friendships and connections. That might be acceptable for some people. Some people might be able to adapt to that kind of life. Even prefer it.

Carey didn't think she could live like this much longer. She felt that tonight, she'd come to the end of her rope. If moving up to Canada didn't solve her problems, she wasn't sure what she'd do.

She felt tears well up in her eyes and swallowed hard, struggling not to cry.

Carey wasn't sure where the animal had come from.

She'd been distracted, lost in her thoughts.

Suddenly…it was just *there*.

Darting out from between the trees. Leaping across the road, right in front of her car.

It looked huge, with wide antlers and long powerful legs, yet it moved with fluid grace, as if in slow motion.

Mesmerized, she sat back and slammed on the brakes. Her seat belt tightened around her body; her mouth hung open. She would have screamed, but there wasn't time. Barely time to take a gasping breath.

It was close. Too close…

She yanked the steering wheel to the left and heard a hoof nick the hood.

The car bounced over the shoulder of the road, then slid down a snowy slope. Carey continued to slam on the brakes, even yanked the emergency brake lever to no avail. She finally shielded her face with one arm, glancing back at her baby daughter, who was still miraculously asleep.

Then the car slowly rolled to a stop, the front end coasting into a tree, the final impact hard enough to jerk her forward and crunch the bumper, but not quite enough to inflate the air bag.

Carey twisted in her seat. "Lindsay? Sweetie?"

Lindsay stared at her wide-eyed, then suddenly started to cry. Her car seat was secure and hadn't budged an inch out of place.

Carey sent up a silent prayer of thanks that they weren't hurt, then clawed at her seat belt, unfastened it and jumped out.

She stood knee-deep in snow, pulled open the back door and crawled in the back to comfort Lindsay. She took the baby from her seat and held her close. The feeling of her small, warm body pressed close was a comfort. She realized she was shaking from the shock. Lindsay soon stopped crying and relaxed against Carey's shoulder.

Carey took a calming breath and tried to remember what she should do. She leaned over and turned on the emergency flashers. Then she wondered if anyone would see them with her car below the embankment.

"We need to call for help," Carey told the baby. "Someone needs to come pull us out of here…wherever here is…"

She picked up her cell phone from the front seat and dialed 911.

An operator answered immediately.

"I've had an accident," Carey began. "My car skidded off the road and hit a tree. I'm alone with a baby. We need some help. Right away…"

Carey tried to remain calm, but just explaining what had happened made her feel desperate and frightened.

"How old is your child, ma'am?"

"Six months, a little girl."

"Is anyone hurt? Any bleeding?"

"No, we're both fine. Just please, send someone to pick us up. I'm afraid that my daughter is going to get frostbite."

"We'll send help right away. Where are you located?"

"I… I'm not sure… I got off the highway at the last exit. Then I turned off the exit ramp… The sign said Greenwood…or Greenbriar…" Carey sighed. "I don't live around here. I was lost and I got off the road to find a gas station…"

"Okay, miss. I have some idea where you might be. Were you traveling north or south?"

"I don't know…" Carey tried hard not to lose her temper.

"I went right at the stop sign…I think."

"Is the car visible from the road…?"

The connection started to break up. Carey spoke quickly.

"I don't know… I…"

Then the phone went dead.

Carey stared at the screen. The battery had run down. She hadn't even realized it was low. She shook it, knowing it wouldn't help at all. She felt so frustrated, she wanted to scream.

Good Lord, this couldn't be happening…

Had she given the operator enough information to find the car? She could hardly say for sure. It was snowing so hard. The windows of the half-buried car were already coated so that she couldn't see out.

It was a holiday. And such a small town. She didn't think there would be many police or EMS workers on duty tonight to come look for her.

It might take a long time. It might take…hours.

What now? Was she stuck here with Lindsay? She couldn't start walking, not in this snow. And where would she walk to? She hadn't seen a single house since she'd turned off the highway.

Or a car or truck passing. She didn't want to leave Lindsay alone even for a few minutes, while she walked up to the road, but she realized she had to. She could tie her scarf to a tree or set out some other distress signal.

She pushed down a wave of panic. If they were stranded for hours, what would she do? She didn't even want to think that far.

Carey secured Lindsay in her seat again, closed the car and headed up the snow-covered slope toward the road. The hill was steep and she thought it was a miracle the car had made it to the bottom in one piece, without either of them being hurt.

That was one lucky break.

She had to tug herself up, pulling on a branch, to get to the road again. Her leather boots with thin soles and heels were not exactly ideal for hiking, but finally, she made it.

She stood at the shoulder of the road and gasped for air, then gasped with alarm as a man ran toward her through the snow. He was big. Very big. With broad shoulders and long legs. He wore a thick parka with the hood pulled up over his head and knee-high boots.

Backlit from the headlights of a car parked down the road, his face was obscured and she couldn't see anything more than his outline.

Carey felt frozen in place and swallowed hard, hoping he was help and not more trouble.

When he finally drew closer she could see from the patches on his jacket that he was a police officer and she breathed a deep sigh of relief.

"Gosh, you got here quickly. I didn't think the 911 operator even knew where I was. Then my phone went dead and…"

He stared at her a moment. "I wasn't sent out to find you. I was just driving home and saw the flashers."

Home to his cozy warm house and a family, who was probably waiting for him to celebrate Christmas Eve, she added silently.

"Thanks for stopping."

"No thanks necessary. Are you all right?"

His voice was deep and even, soothing her ragged nerves.

He took a step closer, staring down at her. "What happened to your car? Did you skid in the snow?"

"An animal jumped out from the woods. I guess it was a deer. I turned, trying to avoid it."

"Are you traveling alone?"

A logical question. Though the way he said it and the way

he was looking at her now made her swallow hard. Made her feel even more isolated…and lonely.

"I have my baby with me. She's down in the car, but she's fine. I left her for a minute so I could put out a distress signal."

The word *baby* had barely left Carey's lips and the officer was in motion. He skidded down the hill easily in his heavy boots, taking the last few yards on his side, without a thought for the snow. He reached the car in a few long loping strides and pulled open the door.

Carey ran behind him. She didn't come down the hill nearly as gracefully and rode most of the way on her bottom.

By the time she reached the car, he had Lindsay out of her seat and handed her up to Carey's waiting arms.

"She looks okay. You bundled her up well."

Then he picked up the extra blanket on the backseat and tucked it around the baby. Carey was surprised. She hadn't even asked him. It was an unexpected, tender gesture.

Lindsay was crying, but he didn't seem to notice. There was something about him, a centered, calm air that seemed as unshakable as a mountain. The complete opposite of how she felt.

"Need anything from the back?" he asked.

"That blue baby bag—" she pointed it out "—and the black duffel…and the car seat, too. I guess."

He scooped up both heavy bags and slung the straps over his shoulders as if they were empty. Then he picked up the car seat. He locked up the car and they headed back toward the road.

When they reached the snowy slope, he put the bags down and turned to her. "Let's leave the bags and seat down here. I'll come back for them. I'll hold the baby if you like and we can go up together."

Carey considered his plan for a moment, then remembered going up the hill the first time and nodded. "All right."

She handed Lindsay over, feeling a tiny, instinctive twinge

of concern. It vanished in an instant once she saw the way her rescuer cradled the baby protectively to his chest.

His strong, gentle embrace was reassuring and a much safer way for Lindsay to travel than if she had carried the baby herself.

He stood by and let her go up first. She started to slip and he was instantly at her side, one strong arm cradling Lindsay to his chest and the other suddenly wrapped around her waist, catching her close before she fell.

He looked down at her. Just about all she could see of his face, covered by his parka hood, were his eyes. Brilliant blue of a summer morning, defying the dark night and falling snow.

She focused on getting up the hill, one slippery step at a time. It was hard to ignore the man beside her. His face was suddenly so close she could feel his warm breath on her cheek. She quickly turned away and stared straight ahead. This was the closest she'd been to anyone in over a year, since Tom had died.

"Careful now, I've got you. Just go slowly."

"I can make it." She tried hard to keep her mind on getting up the hill. The feeling of his arm around her waist and his hard strong body so close next to hers was both distracting…and energizing.

When he reached the top, she gave out a sigh of relief. She was sure he thought she was just happy the trek was over.

He carefully handed the baby over, then went down for the rest of her belongings. She wasn't sure how he could manage the two large bags and car seat in one trip, but moments later, he emerged on the roadside, with the entire load, not even winded.

She followed him to a dark green SUV that was parked down the road. He tossed her bags in the back then secured the baby's seat in the backseat. Carey placed Lindsay in the car seat and fastened the strap.

Then she softly kissed the baby on her forehead and stroked her cheek. Carey was sure she must be hungry and need a diaper change. "Poor sweetheart. I'll take care of you very soon," she promised.

Moments later, she sat up front and the police officer started the vehicle. He pushed back the hood of his parka and she finally had a good look at his face.

He was handsome. Very handsome. The eyes had been a hint. The rest was even better than she'd expected.

His dark hair was cut short, close to his head though not a crew cut. He'd pushed it back, wet from the snow, off his forehead with his hand, emphasizing his lean cheeks and the strong lines of his face, set in a serious expression, as he steered the SUV away from the side of the road and then made a wide U-turn.

They were once again headed in the direction of town, she realized, the same way she was going before she drove off the road.

She pushed back her own hood and ran her fingers through her long golden hair, damp from the snow and feeling even curlier and wilder than usual.

She put her hands up to the air vents to warm them and realized he was watching her, his glance lingering in a way that made her feel self-conscious.

It was a classic male-female glance, a taking inventory sort of look. The same she'd just given him, though he hadn't caught her at it. Or had he? she wondered.

"Feel cold? I can turn up the heat."

Considering the direction of her thoughts, she had to hide a smile. She didn't need it any hotter in here.

"Thanks, I'm okay." She pulled off her wet gloves and stuck them in her pocket. "I don't think you ever told me your name, Officer."

"Ben Martin. You can skip the officer part. I'm off duty. I didn't get your name, either."

"Oh, right. It's Carey Mooreland. And that's Lindsay," she added, glancing at the baby in the backseat.

"She's adorable. I'm glad she wasn't hurt. You're lucky in a way about the snow. It slowed the car down considerably. It could have been a lot worse when you hit that tree."

"Yes, it could have been," Carey had to agree. It definitely could have been worse, though the snow had been a major hindrance to her tonight. If not for the snow, she might be in Canada by now. Or close to it. This man had no idea.

"Is there someone you'd like to call?"

He meant a husband or some significant other, of course.

He was just trying to be helpful. But personal questions still made her nervous.

This question in particular was always a difficult one.

"It's all right. I don't have anyone...waiting for me."

He glanced over at her, then back at the road again. She sensed he was curious, but didn't push her for more information.

"I'm on my way to Portland. To visit a friend," she said simply.

That was the cover story she'd composed for the trip. Just in case anyone asked. Portland was somewhat south of this area, she guessed. Though she wasn't sure how far.

He nodded. His silence made her nervous. Did he believe her? Then she realized he was probably just watching his driving in the snow.

"Looks like you're stuck. At least for the night."

"I guess so. What do you think about the car? Can I call someone to tow it?"

"I'll have them call from the station, though I don't know if the local tow company will get to it tonight. I think all the tow trucks within twenty miles are backed up with calls right now."

Carey hated hearing about delays, though she knew it was

illogical to think her car would be towed during a snow-storm…on Christmas Eve night, no less.

"Where will they bring it?"

"The closest auto body shop is Anderson's, in town. Honest guy. He won't rip you off. Though I'm sure he'll be closed tomorrow. You'll probably have to wait until the day after Christmas for him to take a look at it."

Carey's heart sank. She'd be stuck here two days. Then there would be more time to fix the car. Who knew how long that would take? Every minute seemed precious, to keep a step ahead of her pursuers.

"Is there any other place? Besides the shop in town?"

"There are a few on the highway. But then you'll be paying a lot more for the tow. And I can't say how reliable those places are," he added.

A special radio hung from the bottom of the dashboard, she noticed. He picked up the hand piece and asked someone on the other end to call for a tow truck and told them where to find the car.

Carey agreed to have the car brought to the garage in town. That seemed the easiest solution.

The snow still fell heavily and the drive was slow going.

"You can just drop us off anyplace. At a motel or something."

She wondered where that might be. She'd been watching vigilantly out the window and all she could see was snow… and more snow.

"There's a hotel in town. But it's full up. Relatives that come in for the holidays," he explained.

"Maybe I should call and check. There might be a cancel-lation."

He shook his head. "Trust me. They don't have any rooms free tonight."

He glanced at her, the corner his mouth lifted in the promising start of a smile. She sensed he didn't smile often. She wasn't sure why. Just something about him.

Maybe that was a good thing. He was even better-looking, if possible, when he did. When their eyes met, she forgot for a moment what she'd even asked him.

"I have an inside track. My family owns the place. My mother and sister," he added.

It was hard to picture this hunk of a man with a mother. But of course, he had one, along with a wife and children and all kinds of relatives, waiting for him at some big Christmas party, she suspected.

His hands were covered by thick gloves so she couldn't check to see if he wore a ring. Then she realized her thoughts were going way off on some wacky detour. What did it matter to her if he was married or not?

"There must be someplace else." Carey forced herself back on track. "It doesn't have to be fancy. As long as it's clean…and there's heat."

"There are a few B and Bs around, but they're all full tonight, as well. There's a motel a few towns north. But the highway is closed now and I don't dare risk the ride on the back roads. Besides, that place is going to be booked, too. Especially with this weather."

Carey considered his reply. She didn't argue with him. It was probably true. People traveling tonight would get off the road and stop to stay over, if they had any sense at all.

"How about a hospital? Maybe they could give us a bed for the night."

"The hospital is even farther." Before she could answer, he added, "The usual procedure for emergency shelter is the lockup at the station in town." He paused, his glance taking in her worried expression. "Don't worry. I wouldn't leave you in a jail cell on Christmas Eve. I just…wouldn't."

His gaze met hers for a moment, then he stared back at the road again. Carey felt some indefinable current arc between them. She didn't know what to say.

"What do you think we should do?"

He didn't say anything for a long moment. Carey wondered what his solution was going to be.

"I have plenty of room at my house. We're almost there. And I honestly don't see any other solution."

Carey was surprised by the offer. "Are you sure? I mean…there's nowhere else?"

"Tomorrow there'll be lots of vacancies. But tonight, with this snow, I can't think of anyplace else to bring you. You said all you want is a clean room and some heat. I can guarantee that at least."

"How about your family? Won't they mind?" She phrased the question as diplomatically as she could manage.

"Well, there's Dixie…my dog," he explained. "But she's always happy to see company."

His answer pleased her. She didn't want to stop and figure out why. She didn't want to intrude if he did have a wife and family. That's all, she told herself. It wasn't anything more.

"I realize the situation might be a little disconcerting. I mean, you'd be smart to hesitate. I'm going to call the station. You can talk to my sergeant. Make sure I am who I say. Will that make you feel better about it?"

"All right. I guess that would be the smart thing to do."

Ben picked up the radio handset in the car and a short time later, Carey was listening to his superior wax eloquent on Ben's fine points as a gentleman and an officer. Any doubts at all about his trustworthiness were quickly dispelled. Not that she'd ever really suspected him.

"Thank you, Sergeant. You've been very helpful," Carey said for the second or maybe third time.

Ben suddenly took the radio from her. "Thanks a bunch, Jim.

You make me sound like a cross between a Boy Scout and…an action hero."

"I forgot Sherlock Holmes," the older man laughed into the radio. "Hey, Merry Christmas, pal. See you after the holiday."

"Right, Merry Christmas," Ben said, cutting off the connection.

Ben shook his head, staring straight ahead at the road. Carey thought he looked embarrassed by all the praise. Did she see a slight flush on his lean cheeks, or was it just the cold?

"Satisfied?" he asked finally.

"You sound like the star of the police force."

"Possibly… There are only five of us."

A smile flashed over his rugged features and he met her glance for a moment. She had to smile back. The car suddenly felt very close and dark and…intimate. She took a breath and looked out her window.

"How far to your house?" she asked.

"We're almost there," he said quietly.

That was good news. She was eager to put some distance between herself and her handsome rescuer.

A few moments later, he turned off the road, into a narrow lane. Tree branches, weighed down with snow, arched over the vehicle, creating a frosty tunnel.

The car bumped and struggled through the deep snow, though Ben didn't seem to notice or have any concern that they might get stuck.

Finally a house came into view, a small, neat cabin that appeared to be made of logs, with a covered porch and a sloping, snow-covered roof and stone chimney. The windows in front had wooden shutters and window boxes.

Tall graceful pines surrounded the cabin, their covered branches glistening. Carey was reminded of a house in a picture book; in the darkness and snow, it seemed magical.

"Is that a real log cabin?" she asked as the car came to a stop.

"Yes, it is. Built it myself. With a little help from my friends," he added.

"Quite an accomplishment." She glanced at him. "I'm surprised your boss forgot to mention it."

She smiled at him and he smiled back in a slow way that sent a tingle racing up her spine.

"Good point. I'll remind him." He turned to her. "Let's get inside and warm up."

Ben jumped out first and retrieved her belongings from the cargo area. Carey jumped out and took Lindsay.

As she carefully stepped through the high snow toward the door, she felt Ben's strong, steady grasp on her arm. She glanced at him, but he didn't say anything. Just stood by her until she was up on the porch.

He dropped the load of bags and unlocked the front door, then switched on some lights. A big shaggy dog bounded down the stairs, barking furiously. Carey was glad Ben had given her a warning.

"This must be Dixie," she said, bending forward to let the dog smell her hand.

"How did you guess?" He didn't laugh out loud but his blue eyes sparkled. Carey felt a tingling in her chest.

"Dixie…down. Where are your manners?" The big dog immediately sat, staring up at Ben with adoring brown eyes.

He has a way with women. I hope I'm not looking at him like that, Carey thought.

Dixie sat stiffly, her tail beating the floor. She looked to Carey like a cross between an Australian shepherd…and a pony. But she liked dogs and though this one was doubtlessly curious, she did look friendly.

Ben held on to Dixie's collar while she strained to sniff Carey and say hello. Carey patted the dog's head. Her fur was incredibly soft.

"Hey, Dixie. How are you? I'm sorry if we woke you up," she said softly. "She's sweet," she said to Ben.

"She's a big mush. Once you get to know her. She's probably wondering what you're doing here. I don't have many visitors."

Not many visitors? She imagined this guy had women stacked up at the door, right next to the woodpile. Maybe he was the type who always stayed at the woman's place. So he could make a quick getaway in the morning.

He opened the door and the dog bounded outside. "Just make yourself comfortable. I'll be back in a while. Dixie needs some exercise."

He left the house, closing the door behind him and Carey was suddenly left alone with Lindsay, which was just as well. There was plenty of baby maintenance to perform—a diaper change, a bottle, pajamas, if she could find them.

She gazed around, trying to get her bearings. She stood at the entrance to a large, open living room with a stone fireplace on the far wall. The wide pine plank floor was polished to a mellow glow and covered by woven area rugs.

A long, comfortable-looking couch, covered with kilim pillows, and two big armchairs were arranged in the living room, near the hearth.

In the corner, by a window, she saw a mission-style desk, covered with papers and stacks of books, a laptap in the middle of the mess. All in all, a totally masculine, somewhat messy decor, yet at the same time, very homey looking.

Adjoining the living room, a dining area with a wooden table and ladder-back chairs was separated from the kitchen by an open counter space. There were open rafters across most of the ceiling, which added to the house's rustic feeling.

Carey set the baby down on the couch and took off her jacket, then took off the baby's snowsuit. She found the baby bag and changed Lindsay's diaper. Then she carried her into the kitchen, where she fixed a bottle and heated it in a microwave.

The overstuffed armchairs in front of the fireplace proved as comfortable as they looked. Carey sat with Lindsay in her arms, the baby's body growing as heavy and relaxed as a rag doll as she contentedly sucked down her bottle.

When Lindsay was finished, Carey put the bottle aside, coaxed a burp from her little girl. Then she sat back and gently rocked the baby, cradled against her shoulder.

Lindsay's eyes grew heavy with sleep. She seemed perfectly content. It was always amazing to Carey how flexible babies were. How oblivious. The little girl had no idea of what had nearly happened tonight, how they had come within a heartbeat of being seriously hurt. And she had no notion that they were once again on the run.

Maybe someday she'd tell her daughter what they had been through this past year. When Lindsay was all grown-up and could understand. Carey only hoped when that day came, their lives would be peaceful and happy. Could that ever be? she wondered.

A fleece throw hung on the back of the armchair and Carey slipped it around her shoulders. The house was cozy and warm, but she still felt chilled to her bones and was practically shivering. Still in shock maybe, she realized. And suddenly exhausted, all the adrenaline draining from her body.

She'd been in a panic mode for hours; first, running from Vermont and then, shaken up by the accident. A shudder raced through her slim form. She and Lindsay had been lucky. Maybe Ben Martin had been right. Maybe the snowstorm had been fortunate. One of those things that at first seems an obstacle but turns out to be good luck in disguise?

Her eyes drifted closed, the snug blanket around her shoulders recalling the feeling of Ben's strong arm surrounding her as they climbed up the hill, side by side. He'd just been doing his job, helping an accident victim. She doubted he'd even noticed.

She'd noticed. More than she should have. More than she wanted to admit, even in her private thoughts. The sense of his closeness had somehow made her feel breathless and amazingly serene at the same time. She'd felt as if she could have climbed a mountain beside him. Part of it was feeling safe and protected. A rare feeling for Carey.

The same way she felt now, in his house. Though she knew it was only a temporary illusion. It was a wonderful feeling to let go and let her guard down, just for a few hours.

Just long enough to rest. To get a second wind, she reminded herself. *Before you and Lindsay move on.*

Chapter Two

Carey woke slowly. She realized she'd been dreaming. A frightening dream she had often. She is always alone, walking down an empty street at night. Someone is following her, she turns and can't see anything. She walks faster, then runs. Suddenly, they are right in front of her and reach out to grab her. She can feel a painful cold grip on her body, a touch like ice.

She fights back and screams…

Then wakes up.

"Hey…wake up. You're dreaming. It's okay…"

Her eyes finally opened and she blinked. Ben was crouched near her chair, his hand resting lightly on her shoulder, his face very close. He'd been shaking her awake, she realized.

She sat up suddenly, feeling embarrassed as he stood up and looked down at her.

"You had a bad dream."

She pushed her hair back with her hand. "I guess so... I can't remember it now," she lied.

"I shouldn't have let you sleep in that chair. It doesn't look very comfortable."

"It wasn't the chair," she assured him.

He met her gaze again but didn't answer. He walked over to the stone hearth and tossed another log on the fire. The flames jumped and glowed, filling the room with a sudden flash of light.

"I fixed a little bed for Lindsay. I hope you don't mind. I was afraid she might slip off your lap and I didn't want to wake you."

She sat up suddenly, the blanket falling from her shoulders. Her baby was no longer in her arms. She hadn't even realized it...

"Don't worry. She hasn't gone very far," Ben reassured her.

Carey looked down at her feet and found Lindsay snug and soundly asleep in her car seat, tilted back and covered with a soft blanket.

"Thank you. She looks very comfortable."

He stood up and smiled down at her, looking quietly pleased by her compliment.

"Are you hungry? I made a bite to eat. It isn't much, just what I could find in the refrigerator."

"I could eat anything right now," she admitted.

She hadn't eaten since breakfast. She stood up and followed him to the kitchen, forcing herself not to make a mad dash.

A few minutes later, she was seated at the table beside Ben, relishing spoonfuls of thick, hot beef noodle soup and eyeing the grilled cheese sandwich he'd set down beside her bowl.

Neither of them spoke and Carey forced herself to eat at a slow, polite pace.

"This is great soup," she said between spoonfuls. "It tastes homemade."

"My freezer is stocked with takeout containers from the hotel restaurant. Guess I'm the best-fed single guy in town."

And probably the most chased after, Carey silently added for him. But the stocked freezer explained one reason why none of the local single females had caught him yet.

Carey did wonder at the rest of the story.

"I made the sandwich. Just don't look too closely," he warned.

Carey glanced at the grilled cheese, golden on one side, burned to a crisp on the other.

"Not a problem. I'm so hungry, I'll eat anything."

"A clean room, some heat…eats anything you put down in front of her. You're not very hard to please, are you?"

She stared down at her plate and didn't answer. She had her reasons these days for setting low standards. Though she'd never really been fussy or demanding. It just wasn't her nature.

"It makes life easier," she said finally, forcing a small smile.

"It does," he agreed. "Though not everyone sees it that way."

He didn't say more. A shadow passed over his expression, dimming his brilliant eyes. She wondered what he was remembering. Some other woman who had sat here once, right where she was sitting now? Some woman who had been difficult to please?

Carey took a few bites of her sandwich. It wasn't bad at all. Not nearly as bad as it looked. Ben rose and took the soup bowls away.

"Would you like some coffee?"

"Coffee would be great. Just black is fine for me."

"No frills. I should have guessed that." His voice was serious, but Carey noticed a teasing light in his eye. He poured out the two mugs of coffee and carried them into the living room so that Carey could check on the baby.

Lindsay was still sleeping soundly in her makeshift bed.

Carey sat down on the floor next to her and stared into the fire. Ben put another log on the burning pile and stirred up the embers until the fire flared up, bright and strong.

He stretched out on the floor not too far from her. Leaning on one arm, he sipped his coffee and stared into the hearth.

Carey had been watching the fire, but now, could hardly take her eyes off her host. He looked so long and lean, so relaxed... and sexy. She hugged her knees to her chest and took a bracing sip of her coffee.

"Have you lived around here long?" Her voice came out in a croak and she hoped he didn't notice.

Okay, so she didn't sound like the most witty conversationalist, but she was eager to break the heavy silence that had fallen between them.

"I've lived here most of my life. I had two years in the navy and then went to college in North Carolina. I lived down there for a while. But finally, I came back to Maine."

"All those mild winters start to wear on you?"

A half smile played about the corners of his mouth. A dimple creased his cheek and tiny lines fanned out at the corners of his eyes. She hadn't noticed that before.

"That was part of it. No challenge. And it never felt like Christmas."

Carey had spent the holidays in the Caribbean once. Her late husband's idea. Ben was right. It hadn't felt like Christmas at all.

"I came back three years ago. My father was sick and my folks needed my help."

She wasn't surprised. He seemed like the type who would do the right thing. Put aside his own needs to help someone he loved.

"When did he pass away?" she asked quietly.

"About a year after I returned." She heard the note of loss in his voice and it struck a chord within her. That was something else they had in common.

"But you stayed."

He shrugged. "It's a small town, but I guess it suits me. For now, anyway."

Maybe with his father gone, his mother and sister relied on him even more. But she sensed he was too private—or too modest—to admit it.

"I get to be the star of the Greenbriar police force," he added, a sparkle returning to his eyes.

"So I've heard." She met his glance and smiled. She didn't mean to flirt with him…but it suddenly felt as if she was.

"What about you?" he asked curiously.

The light moment was suddenly gone. She pulled back into herself like a turtle retreating into its shell.

"You said you were headed to Portland. Where are you coming from?"

She couldn't stray too far from the truth. Her car had Vermont plates. Surely he'd noticed. He was a policeman. But she did need to protect herself, in case those who pursued her ever found this man and asked him questions.

"Burlington." She gave the name of a town miles on the opposite side of the state from Blue Lake. Then, realizing that a route from Burlington to Portland wouldn't have taken her through this area, she added, "I went up to Freeport to visit a relative. A great-aunt. She… She wanted to see the baby."

Carey smiled and tucked a strand of hair behind her ear, trying to cover a sudden fit of nerves.

"So your friends in Portland, are they expecting you for Christmas?"

Carey shrugged. "More or less. I'm really going there for a job. They own a store and need some help. Someone they can trust."

Did she have to add that last embellishment? Keep it simple, Carey. That was the trick to getting away with all these fabrications.

Stick to your story. If anyone asked—she was going to Portland because a friend had offered her a job in his store, a clothing store. Period.

Ben sipped his coffee. She hoped he was finished with his questions. Under other circumstances, having such an attractive man asking all these questions about her would have been a real ego boost. Tonight it was nerve-racking.

"What sort of work do you do?"

She shrugged. "I've tried just about everything. I've been a waitress, a cabdriver, a receptionist, a dog walker…I've worked in department stores. I've worked in a flower shop. I liked that, but my allergies got to me. I've handed out free samples in supermarkets. Once I had to dress up as a giant cookie, in a shopping mall…" She paused. "Do you really want to hear more?"

"Is there more?" He smiled, looking impressed.

"More than I want to remember." She paused, not knowing how much private information she wanted to disclose. Or how honest she dared to be with him about her real history. "I took some of those jobs working my way through college. I was studying literature. But I really wanted to be an actress. I went to New York for a while and did all the cattle-call auditions. That sort of thing. It didn't work out for me, so I went back home."

He gave her a thoughtful look. "I'm sure it's a tough business. Very competitive."

"Yes, it was. I don't think I was thick-skinned enough. Or maybe, I lacked in the ambition department."

He considered her words for a moment. "You're definitely not lacking in the looks department."

His gaze met hers and held it. She felt the heat rush to her cheeks and hoped he didn't notice. Finally, she looked away, staring at the fire again.

"That's nice of you to say."

"It's just the truth."

Carey felt self-conscious. The way he was looking at her made heat rise to her cheeks. She hoped he thought it was just the fire.

"So, you went back home. Where is that?" he prodded.

She started to say, "Cleveland," then caught herself.

"Scranton, Pennsylvania. Just outside of the city actually," she embellished. "A small town called Wilkes Barre."

"You grew up there?" he asked.

She nodded and forced a smile. She felt her heart beating so loudly, she was almost certain he could hear it. He was a policeman. Couldn't he tell that everything she'd told him was a bald-faced lie? Well, maybe not everything…but enough of it.

She hated living like this and doubly hated the man who had brought her to this point, a point as low as he was himself. She knew it was wrong to hate another person. To wish them ill. But Quinn…

He wasn't even a person. He was a heartless, conscience-less…monster.

She looked over at Ben, at his expression—kind, serious, interested. She had the sudden, insane urge to tell him every-thing. How she had been so vulnerable and easily exploited after Tom died. So naive and easily taken in and now, how she'd found herself stuck in a nightmare. One that would never end.

Would he understand? Would he try to turn her in…or try to help her?

"You look…upset. Am I asking too many questions?" His gaze found hers and held it. "I'm sorry. A policeman's habit."

The urge to pour out her heart nearly overwhelmed her. Then suddenly, she stepped back from the edge and got control of herself.

"It's okay. I'm just tired… My husband died a little over a year ago. The holidays are hard."

That wasn't entirely a lie. Though if Tom were still alive Carey doubted they would still be married. After a whirlwind courtship, they had never been happily married and were about to separate when she'd found out she was pregnant. They decided to stick it out until the baby came and give it one more try.

Then Tom had died and she was left a widow, three months pregnant.

"That's tough. I'm sorry," he said sincerely. "Was it sudden?"

Carey nodded. "An accident at a construction site."

Tom had worked in the front office of Quinn's construction company, a project manager. He'd been at a building site, gone up on scaffolding and had fallen off. He'd died instantly from his injuries. The autopsy found a high level of alcohol in his blood and there were witnesses who claimed he'd been drinking at lunchtime. Their insurance company was absolved from paying her anything more than a small death benefit.

She didn't mind for herself, but there was the baby to think of. That's when Quinn had stepped in. Swooped in, more like it.

When she'd first met Quinn, she'd thought he was a kind man. It was a dark time and, with no close family to help her, she'd taken the help Quinn had so generously offered. Money to tide her over until she was ready to work and a good job as a bookkeeper in the main office. Perhaps he'd been afraid that Carey was going to sue him for responsibility for the accident, but she wasn't that type of person. Besides, lawsuits and lawyers cost money and she needed every dollar to support herself and Lindsay. Her pregnancy with Lindsay was difficult. She was sick all the time. She didn't have any close family to help her and he'd insisted on helping her financially until she was able to work again.

Carey was alone in the world. Her father had left when she was very young. She'd never really known him and didn't know

now if he was dead or alive. Her mother had raised her in a loving home, though they'd never had much money. She'd been very proud when Carey graduated college and had high hopes for her only daughter. But she was killed in a car accident a few months later. Carey was devastated.

She could see now that was part of the reason she'd married Tom so quickly. He'd swept her off her feet, acting as if he couldn't live without her. But once they were married, he'd grown bored and restless very quickly.

Looking back, Carey could see that she'd been very naive and vulnerable. Easily taken in by Tom and, later, by Quinn, who was older. He'd acted very fatherly toward her, though sometimes taking too great an interest in her personal life, wanting to have too much control.

After Lindsay was born, he offered her a job at his company, her office steps from his own. A good salary, flexible hours and she was even able to bring the baby with her whenever necessary. Quinn didn't mind.

He doted on Lindsay and bought her every kind of toy and stuffed animal imaginable. He seemed to enjoy having her in the office. Carey thought of him as a loving uncle. Or even a father figure. She'd been very stupid and blind, never realizing how Quinn really thought of himself.

As Lindsay's future stepfather.

No matter how gently or diplomatically she'd try to explain that she wasn't interested in that kind of relationship, he still held out hopes. He still acted as if someday she'd change her mind. He was waiting for her to get over Tom's death. Then her feelings for him would change, he'd say.

The only thing Carey wanted to change was her job. But it wasn't that easy. She began to fear his reaction if she resigned. His reprisals to business rivals who he believed "crossed him" were chilling. Carey began to feel stalked by his obsessive interest, to be truly afraid of him and felt a prisoner under his ever-watchful eye.

She could save a little money out of her weekly paycheck, but never enough to escape. Still, she scrimped and saved for her freedom, knowing she could never tell him outright that she was leaving town. She'd hinted at it once and his reaction had been frightening. Of course, he was sorry afterward. So miserable and contrite, leaving a dozen roses on her desk, a snowsuit and stuffed toys for Lindsay, begging her forgiveness. Quinn needed help. Serious help for his mood swings and temper tantrums. But who in his circle had the guts to tell him? Not Carey.

Finally, Quinn went too far. She discovered that he was meddling in the books and tax records, in ways that were unethical, even illegal. She was afraid of his reaction, but confronted him anyway. Her conscience demanded it. As she expected, he flew into a rage, and threatened her.

He claimed she was culpable, too. She was handling a lot of the financial records, wasn't she? She could never leave now because he'd use the improprieties against her.

Carey pretended to heed his warnings and played along, promising that she'd let him judge what was best for the business. But when she had a chance, she scraped up what little money she could, accepted help from friends and ran as far away from Quinn as she could manage.

She went to Chicago, figuring it would be the best place to disappear into a crowd. She also had a college friend who helped her find a job and get settled under a new identity. Her life was falling into place again.

The friends back in Ohio who helped her get away and stay hidden were Paul Newton and his wife, Nora. Paul was one of Quinn's site foremen and kept Carey informed about Quinn's activities. Quinn had been looking for her, Paul reported, but after a few months when her trail went cold, he seemed to give up or be distracted by more immediate concerns.

A few weeks ago, Paul reported that Quinn's business practices, along with a mortgage company that he dealt with often, had come under investigation. He was indicted as part of a ring, charged with rigging fake mortgages and defrauding the bank of millions.

Carey learned that investigators for the prosecution were looking for her. They wanted her testimony and maybe even believed she'd been involved in the illegal deals, too.

Carey knew if she dared to come out of hiding and profess her innocence, and testify against Quinn, he would find a way to take revenge on her…and Lindsay. While her conscience urged her to offer her testimony, her instincts as a mother overruled. She didn't dare risk putting her baby in danger.

She didn't trust the authorities to believe her. Or protect her. The man was more than obsessive, he was insane. What if he wasn't found guilty? Or wasn't given a long prison sentence? He would come after her for sure. She couldn't take that chance. So now she had both the legal authorities looking for her and Quinn's private investigators.

If she stopped to think about it too much, it was hard to function…to keep going. To do what she had to do to survive…

Ben's voice broke into her rambling thoughts. She could tell from his expression he thought she must have been lost in thoughts of her late husband.

"The holidays can be hard if you're alone," he said finally. "Everywhere you look, everyone seems so happy. If you don't feel that way, you think something must be wrong with you. You feel so…out of sync."

That was exactly the way she felt. Though in her case, it was even more complicated. He seemed to understand and feel the same. She wondered if he had any plans to celebrate Christmas

Day or would avoid it by going to work. But she didn't feel comfortable asking him.

"Would you like some more coffee?"

"No, thanks." Carey shook her head and sat up.

It was wonderful to sit with him like this, talking and staring at the fire. She worried that if she sat much longer she'd get so relaxed, she'd end up giving all her secrets away.

"I think I'd better turn in. Before I fall asleep again in your living room."

"You're welcome to sack out anyplace you like. But I did put your things in the guest room and made up the bed with clean sheets. You should be comfortable there."

He rose from the floor in a quick, agile motion, then stretched down his hand to her. "Come on, I'll show you."

Carey at first ignored his help, then reached up and put her hand in his. She needed a tug. She was bone-tired after her ordeal today and could barely move.

She came to her feet and they suddenly stood face-to-face, so close she could feel his breath stirring her hair.

He gazed down at her, studying her face. She tried hard to avoid looking into his eyes, but it was impossible.

He lifted one hand and touched her soft curly hair, pushing a strand back from her cheek. His hand lingered there for a moment, cupping her cheek. Carey knew he was about to kiss her and knew she ought to step away. But somehow, her feet wouldn't move, stuck firmly in place. Somehow, her gaze wouldn't break away from his as his head dipped and his face came even closer.

Her lips parted and she took in a deep breath, her eyes starting to drift closed.

Lindsay's soft whimper broke the silence. They both stepped back and looked down at the baby. She'd been sleeping so peacefully all this time, Carey hadn't fussed over her at all.

Carey knelt and checked the baby's diaper, which was dry. Then she patted Lindsay's back, murmuring softly to her. The baby was soon fast asleep again.

Ben leaned down and spoke in a whisper. "I'll carry the car seat to your room. No need to wake her."

"Good idea," Carey whispered back.

Ben lifted the basket easily, baby and all. He headed for the stairway and Carey followed.

At the top of the stairs he turned left and led her to a small bedroom at the end of the hallway. A milk glass lamp on a small table by the bed cast the room in a soft glow. A full-size bed pushed against one wall took up most of the space. It was covered with a white-and-blue quilt with a traditional wedding ring pattern, a striped wool blanket folded at the foot of the bed and fluffy pillows.

A small white painted dresser and a rocking chair were the only other furnishings. The ceiling slanted with the eaves of the roof above, lending the room a cozy, warm feeling.

Carey saw that Ben had already brought up her duffel bag and other belongings and left them at the foot of the bed.

"Well…here you are. The bathroom is the next door down, on the right. My room is at the other end of the hall. If you need anything, just call me."

As he spoke, he started to back out of the room. Carey watched from where she stood by the bed. He suddenly seemed nervous and she could guess why. The sight of the big empty bed made her acutely conscious of their attraction, too, and how he had just nearly kissed her… And now that they were alone together in this house all night long…

She imagined herself and Ben, lost in a rapturous embrace, rolling around on the big soft bed… Then she blinked to dispel the image.

Ben had been speaking, but she'd lost track.

"…well, good night. See you in the morning." He stood in the doorway, his hands dug into the front pockets of his jeans, filling the space with his big body.

She started to take a step toward him, then decided it was best to say good-night from a safe distance.

"Thanks again for all your help. I don't know what I would have done if you hadn't found us."

He shook his head, embarrassed at her gratitude. "I'm just glad that you and Lindsay are okay. Good night, Carey…Merry Christmas."

The soft, deep tone of his voice seemed to hold a note of longing, a single note that touched something deep within her.

"Good night, Ben." She met his gaze briefly before he closed the door.

Chapter Three

Carey sat down on the edge of the bed. She listened as Ben's footsteps faded down the hallway, followed by Dixie's soft tread. Then she heard a door open and close.

What had gotten into her tonight?

She barely knew the man and here she was, ready to just… lose all control if he'd so much as kissed her.

It had to be the accident and being rescued by him. Feeling saved and protected. It had to be this cozy house and the spell cast by the firelight. She'd been fending for herself for a long time. She was tired and vulnerable. Especially tonight.

But she couldn't let her guard down. Not even with a man like Ben. Especially not a man like him. One who was so honest and straight.

Carey dug through her purse and pulled out her cell phone, then found the power cord in her duffel and plugged it into the wall and the other end, into her phone.

She flipped it open and turned it on. There was a message and she recognized the number. Paul and Nora Newton. She dialed her mailbox and listened to the call.

"Carey, it's Paul. I just wanted to check in with you, see where you're at. Nora sends her love. We know you're not having much of a Christmas, but we're thinking of you. Give the baby a kiss for us and call when you can. We hope that you're at least safe and warm."

The familiar voice was a comfort. Paul and Nora were almost like parents to her. Yet she wondered if there was something more Paul wanted to tell her. Did he have some news about Quinn?

She'd call back tomorrow and let him know she was stuck in Maine for a few days. She hoped the delay wouldn't help Quinn's investigators catch up to her.

Lindsay was still sound asleep in the seat, which now sat on the bed, close to the wall. Carey leaned over and stroked the baby's soft cheek with her fingertip.

They were definitely safe and warm here, in Ben Martin's house. At least for tonight.

Carey woke slowly from a deep sleep. At first, she didn't remember where she was. Then it all came back, the accident and Ben Martin. Sitting in his kitchen and then by the fire. Nearly kissing him… She remembered that very clearly.

She peered into the car seat that sat beside her on the bed. Lindsay was still asleep. She looked like a little angel. The makeshift cradle must be very comfortable, Carey thought.

The bedroom was filled with the soft glow of morning sunlight reflected off the freshly fallen snow. Carey got up and pulled back the curtains. The snowfall had ended sometime during the night and the sky was clear blue and cloudless. Every inch outdoors was covered with white.

Mostly, Carey saw tall pine trees. Out in front of the cabin, she saw the large green SUV. Someone—Ben, of course—had already shoveled in front of the cabin, cleaned off the vehicles and shoveled a car-wide path leading up to his private lane. She wondered if they would have trouble getting out of here today. She hoped not.

Lindsay began to stir and Carey picked her up, then took care of her. She set the basket in a safe place in the bathroom while she showered and dressed in jeans and a soft blue sweater.

Her long curly hair was a sight, but she didn't want to take the time to wash it. She swept it up in a loose knot and clipped it at the back of her head. She didn't have any makeup handy, but did find some lip gloss in the bottom of her bathroom kit and swiped it on.

She would have liked to look nicer across the breakfast table this morning. But what was the difference? Ben's interested glances and rare smiles might give her ego a boost. But nothing could come of it. She'd be leaving here in a day or two and would never see him again. She had to remember that. Though each time she stared into those blue eyes, she seemed to fall headfirst, into the deep end.

She carried Lindsay downstairs in her basket. The smell of coffee and something cooking led her to the kitchen.

Ben stood at the stove, his back turned toward her. He wore a dark blue Henley shirt over jeans. The soft knit fabric emphasized his broad shoulders and back. The worn jeans draped his lean hips and long legs like an advertisement for masculine sex appeal.

He turned to her, taking her in from head to toe with a sweeping glance. Carey was glad she'd gone for the lip gloss.

"Merry Christmas." His voice was deep and quiet. Almost serious.

"Merry Christmas, Ben…I almost forgot," she confessed.

"I didn't have time to get you anything. So I made you some pancakes and bacon."

He flipped a pancake with a long spatula, then glanced over his shoulder at her.

"The homemade gifts are always the best. Especially if they're edible. Anything I can do to help?"

"I don't think so. There's coffee in that pot. The pancakes will be done in a minute. How's Lindsay this morning? Did she have a good sleep?"

"Straight through the night. She slept much later than usual, too."

So did I, Carey realized, glancing at the clock. She felt embarrassed for coming down so late, while Ben had been up and about, shoveling snow and cooking pancakes.

Carey made Lindsay a bottle of milk and heated it in the microwave, then fed the baby some cereal and a jar of peaches. The baby was finished with her breakfast at just about the same time Ben brought the platters of food to the table.

Carey balanced Lindsay on her knee as she fixed herself a dish and started eating. "Mmm…these are good. How do you get them to come out so thin?"

Carey wasn't very good in the kitchen and was impressed by anyone who could cook.

"The great chefs never tells their secrets." He smiled slightly, then sat back and took a sip of coffee. "I owed you for the burned grilled cheese."

"The grilled cheese was fine." She shrugged. "But these are…much better."

She dipped a forkful of pancake in a puddle of syrup on her plate and popped it into her mouth. These really were the best pancakes she'd had in a long time. She glanced around the kitchen and could see he'd gone to some trouble to fix such a nice breakfast. She would insist on cleaning up.

Then she'd insist on leaving.

He'd gone out of his way to make her feel comfortable in his home and she didn't feel right causing any more work for him. He had his own life, his own obligations and plans for the holiday. Though he'd only mentioned his family, she was sure that there must be a woman in the picture, somewhere.

"I'd better call some hotels this morning and see if I can find a room," Carey said suddenly. She glanced at him, but he didn't show any reaction.

"I can take you to the Greenbriar Inn in town."

"The inn your family runs?"

"That's right." He dabbed his mouth with a paper napkin. "I called this morning and told my mother about you. She has plenty of guests checking out today. She's going to find a nice room for you and Lindsay."

Carey didn't know what to say. He thought of everything, didn't he? "I appreciate your help, Ben. Once again."

"It wasn't much. Just a phone call."

"I hope it's not out of your way to take us there? Maybe I should call a cab."

He leaned back in his chair and laughed. "There are only two taxis in this town, Carey, and neither are pulled by reindeer, so I think you're stuck riding with me. Some of the roads won't be plowed, but we'll get through. I'm going to the inn later. It's not any trouble to take you."

"I thought you might be working today."

"I have the day off. No excuse to miss the family Christmas party."

The corner of his mouth lifted in a small smile, but Carey sensed that given half a chance, he would have liked to skip the family party.

"Is it a big group?"

"Big enough. Aunts, uncles, cousins… We have a big

family on both sides and they all assume that since my mother runs a hotel with a huge dining room, she should host all the holidays. She complains," he confessed, "but I don't think she'd ever give it up, even if someone offered to take over."

It sounded like a very big party. Carey wasn't surprised that Ben had mixed feelings about being part of it. He didn't seem the type who enjoyed big parties. She could already tell that much about him.

"How about you? Does your family have parties on the holidays?"

Carey shook her head. "My folks are both gone. My dad died when I was in high school and my mother, just a few years ago. My parents would entertain a few relatives and friends at Christmastime. But it was usually pretty quiet. I do have some nice memories of those days," she said wistfully. "Special presents. Baking cookies with my mom. Singing Christmas carols. That sort of thing…"

She'd never told anyone that, Carey realized. Not even Tom. But no one else had ever asked, had they?

Ben's expression was thoughtful. "You're pretty much alone in the world right now, aren't you?"

Carey shrugged, making light of his question. "Oh, I wouldn't say that. There's Lindsay," she said, glancing down at the baby. Lindsay was the joy of her heart. She'd do anything for her. "We have each other. We're independent types," she added.

"I can see that," he said quietly.

She felt the conversation growing too serious. "What time do you want to leave for town?" she asked suddenly.

"In about an hour." He glanced at his watch. "That should be enough time, even with the snow."

Carey rose and picked up some dirty dishes.

"I can do that," Ben said.

"Sorry, my turn. You made breakfast," she reminded him. "This will be my Christmas present."

She glanced at him and caught a rare smile. He crossed his arms over his broad chest and watched her work.

"It was this…or a tie. You don't seem the tie type, though."

His smile grew wider. "You're right. I'm not."

He was anything but. You'd have to be blind not to see that, Carey reflected. She worked quickly, focusing on her tasks.

He watched her for a moment more, then started to help her. She didn't argue with him, though she felt a bit light-headed from his nearness in the small kitchen. She was relieved when they were done and she was able to take Lindsay upstairs again and get ready to leave for the inn.

The short stay at Ben's cabin had worked an amazing effect. She felt so relaxed, as if she'd been on a weeklong vacation. She'd eaten well, slept well and her pressing worries had suddenly seemed very distant. All the voices in her head were muffled by the snowfall and her mind totally distracted by her handsome, compelling host.

Now as they drove toward town, Carey felt all her cares rushing in again. But it was Christmas, she reminded herself. Even if she wasn't going to celebrate the day, she could at least give herself a day off from worrying.

She watched the snow-covered scenery pass by. It all looked different in the daylight. Now she could see the road she'd driven down did have a few houses scattered here and there. Or at least, roadside mailboxes and narrow lanes that seemed to indicate life up in the woods. The houses soon became more visible and frequent. She realized they were coming into town.

Greenbriar wasn't even a full dot on the map. But up close, it was a pretty and surprisingly lively looking place, with shops, restaurants, a post office, movie theater and a town hall. A lot like the town she'd left in Vermont—Blue Lake. But a bit bigger, she thought. The village was decorated beautifully, with wreaths on shop windows and garlands strung across Main Street.

Ben pulled up to a huge, Victorian mansion that faced the village green. A wooden sign in front read Greenbriar Inn in gold lettering. The three-story building was painted a muted rose color with burgundy, forest-green and golden-yellow trim.

The first floor was circled by a wide, columned porch and the second floor had a large balcony in front. The porch was draped with pine garlands and wreaths hung in all the windows on the first and second floor, each with long satin bows. A huge pine wreath decorated the front entranceway, double doors arched on top.

All in all, Carey could rarely remember ever seeing such an amazing old building.

"Here we are." Ben parked and turned off the engine.

"Wow. It's fantastic." She turned to him. "Did you grow up in there?"

He nodded slowly. "I always wished we lived in a 'real' house. Though I certainly found a lot of ways to get in trouble living in a hotel while other kids never had the opportunity."

"I'd never take you for the mischievous type, Ben," she said honestly.

He smiled and pocketed his keys. "You don't know me very well. Yet."

His words held a promise. Or was it a dare? One she'd like to take him up on. She did want to know him better. But that wasn't going to happen. Carey sighed and gathered her belongings.

She had to stay in town a few days for her car, but it would probably be best to avoid seeing much more of him. She already knew she was amazingly attracted and could easily have feelings for him. Very easily, she thought.

Ben got out and started to unload the car. There were bags

of gifts for his family and Carey's luggage. They managed to get everything up on the porch and then, into the hotel foyer. Carey couldn't help gazing around at the decor, as Ben did most of the heavy lifting.

The hotel lobby was not large, with several sitting areas, but elegantly decorated. A registration desk stood at one end of the room. A woman rushed out from a doorway behind the desk. It appeared to lead to a small office.

Her expression brightened at the sight of Carey and Lindsay and Carey could tell immediately she was Ben's mother. Her bright blue eyes were a giveaway. Her dark hair was threaded with silver, pulled back in a neat upswept hairstyle. She wore pearl earrings, a cream-colored scoop-neck sweater and a black velvet skirt that came down below her knees. She smiled as she walked out from behind the desk.

"Merry Christmas. You must be Carey and Lindsay."

Carey nodded. "That's us."

"I'm Ben's mother, Thea." She stuck out her hand and Carey shook it. "Ben told me about your accident. How frightening for you. It was so lucky that you and the baby weren't hurt."

"Yes, we were lucky."

Ben came back inside with more gift bags, the last of them. "Merry Christmas, Mom." He leaned over and kissed his mother on the cheek.

"Merry Christmas, Ben."

"I see you've met Carey. I can bring her things up if her room is ready."

"That would be a help. We're very shorthanded today. I gave the staff the day off, of course." She started walking across the lobby and Carey followed. Ben picked up Carey's bags and also followed.

"I've put you in a nice room on the second floor. It's really a double, with room for the baby. It has a lovely view of the green."

They climbed a stairway up two short flights and came out in a wide hall. Thea led them to a nearby door and opened it with a key she had in her pocket. The door seemed to stick for a moment and she pulled it toward her and wiggled the knob.

"Oh, dear. Ben, you'll have to fix this when you come next time." She glanced at her son as the door finally swung open.

"Just put it on the list." His tone was quiet and resigned.

Carey didn't realize he helped out here, but it did make sense when she thought about it.

Ben stepped aside and let his mother and Carey walk in first. The sticky lock was soon forgotten.

The room was large and tastefully decorated with blue-and-white-striped drapes over sheers and a matching satin bed set. More of a suite, Carey noticed, with a separate sitting area. Thea opened a large wooden armoire that contained a TV and small refrigerator.

"It's lovely," Carey said. She stepped over to the window and pulled the curtain aside. Long French doors led to a balcony and framed a view of the snow-covered village green.

Ben came in and set down the luggage. "Very nice. I've always liked this view."

Thea smiled at him in an amused way. "Glad you approve. I found a portable crib for the baby. It's down in the office. Ben can bring it up for you later," she said to Carey. "We'll let you unpack and freshen up. Come down to the party anytime you're ready. Ben will save a place for you."

The party? Did she mean their family party? Carey didn't plan on joining Ben and his family today. For one thing, she didn't want to intrude and be even more trouble. For another, it was far easier for her to keep to herself and not be forced to answer a lot of questions…and tell a lot of lies.

His mother seemed to read her thoughts easily. Was her expression so transparent?

Thea took a step closer and rested her hand lightly on Carey's arm. "Of course you'll join us. You must. We aren't serving any food in the restaurant today, for one thing. Nothing in town is open, either. You have to come down and eat. And we'd love to have you. That's what Christmas is all about."

Carey smiled at her, but didn't seem convinced. Thea glanced at her son, looking for some help.

"I always feel out of sync at these things and you can keep me company." He stared down into her eyes, his blue eyes working their special magic, melting her willpower.

He'd changed from his snow-shoveling, pancake-making clothes before they'd left the house and looked very handsome in a slim-fitting black pullover and a dark gray sport jacket.

"My mother is only trying to scare you about the food. If you really don't want to come down, I'll bring something up for you."

There was definitely safety in numbers, Carey decided. No telling what would happen if she stayed up here with Ben providing room service.

"Of course I'll come. Thank you for the invitation, Mrs. Martin."

"It's Thea…and you're very welcome." She smiled slightly, then glanced over at Ben. "We're still on the appetizers. No rush. I'll see you two downstairs."

Thea closed the door behind her but Ben stayed, Carey noticed. "Don't you need to go down and see your family? I won't be very long," she told him.

"I can wait. I'm afraid if I leave you up here, you might be tempted to hide out all day."

His suspicions were correct. The way he'd read her mind made her smile.

"Is that a law around here? No one can be alone on Christmas?"

"It *might* be," he teased her back. "You don't want to end up in the lockup after all. Not when you've just landed in such a cushy spot."

"You're right. That wouldn't be very smart." She opened her bag, took out some clothes and put them in a drawer. "Your mother is very nice. Very…hospitable."

"She's a natural at making people feel welcome. Maybe that's what keeps this place in business after all."

"Is there some problem?"

Ben shrugged. He picked up a stuffed dog, then waved it at Lindsay, who was lying on the bed. "The inn hasn't been doing that well since my father died. She's had to let a lot of the help go. It's hard for her. I try to help, with repairs and the outdoor work when I can and my sister works here, too. She does all the food service. But it's still a lot of responsibility for one person. Sometimes she talks about selling it. But I'd hate to see that happen," he said honestly.

Carey didn't know what to say. She'd heard there were always complications and tensions when a family ran a business together. She guessed Ben's family was not immune, though he seemed very easygoing.

It didn't seem the time to talk about these private matters. Carey didn't want to seem as if she was prying, either. Lindsay soon got bored with the stuffed toy and Ben picked her up, talking softly to her while she patted his head with her hands.

Carey liked the way he handled the baby. His strong but gentle touch touched her heart. That was just the way she'd imagined a good stepfather would treat her little girl. If she ever found a good stepfather for Lindsay…which right now seemed highly unlikely.

Carey found a lipstick and swiped on a fresh coat, then fluffed up her hair with her fingers and put on a pair of silver hoop earrings she'd found in her makeup bag.

She definitely wasn't dressed for a party. This morning, she'd pulled on a blue velour hooded top with a cream-colored camisole underneath, jeans and boots. She wondered if she should at least change to a dressy blouse and put on some jewelry.

Ben stood near the door, watching her. "Don't worry, Carey. You look…perfect."

She glanced at him, then looked away. "No, I don't, but thanks," she said, smiling at him.

Perfect? She knew it was just a word. Something anyone might say. He didn't really mean anything by it. Still, the tone of his voice and the way he looked at her made her feel something positively electric between them, like a bolt of heat lightning. "Let's go. I don't want to keep your family waiting for us." She scooped up her bag, suddenly eager to join the party downstairs.

Hanging around a hotel room with this man was not a great idea. Lindsay was not much of a chaperone.

Chapter Four

The family gathering was just as Ben had described it. Maybe even bigger and noisier, Carey thought, with everyone talking, eating and laughing at once.

Carey knew that if she hadn't felt the gentle pressure of Ben's hand on her back, guiding her into the dining room, she would have made some polite excuse and run back upstairs again.

Thea's guests sat at a long table that stretched from one end of the large room to the other. The room was beautifully decorated for the holiday, with arrangements of red-and-white roses mixed with holly and trailing ivy, white candles of various sizes, glowing everywhere, and a large Christmas tree at the room's far end, surrounded by piles of gifts.

A gang of children, too excited to eat, ran around chasing each other. They had clearly started the day in their best clothes, but now shirttails were flapping, satin sashes were trailing and ponytails had come undone.

They looked as if they were having a great time, as children know how to do instinctively at these kinds of parties. Before too long the baby in her arms would be running with the pack, Carey thought wistfully. Though they would not be part of any big holiday reunions like this one.

Thea had saved seats for Carey and Ben, and also set up a high chair for the baby. Ben led them to their places and they sat down. He introduced Carey to those seated nearby, mostly married cousins and aunts, from what Carey could gather. She tried hard but couldn't keep all the names straight in her head.

Everyone seemed very welcoming and there was a great deal of talk about the snowfall, their different routes traveling to Greenbriar, and about the dinner, which emerged slowly from the kitchen, each course more delicious than the next.

It seemed that Ben's sister, Luanne, had prepared the entire meal and was busy working in the kitchen throughout the festivities.

The menu was extensive—with a salad course, roast goose, baked ham and beef tenderloin, all kinds of side dishes, garlic mashed potatoes, sweet potatoes and corn bread stuffing. There were platters of roast vegetables, asparagus, stuffed mushrooms and string beans with almonds.

Carey hoped the chef would emerge at some point. She wanted to meet the talent behind such a wonderful Christmas feast. She did see Ben's mother, Thea, running in and out of the swinging doors, carrying out more and more dishes laden with food.

Carey didn't feel pressured to socialize and mostly sat quietly, just watching everyone. It was a lively, warm gathering and she thought Ben was lucky to be part of such a big family. It was some-thing she'd missed growing up and missed in her life now, too.

Ben sat on her left, talking mostly to a cousin about his own age named Jeff, who sat across the table. Jeff was a lawyer who lived in Connecticut. He and Ben seemed to have a good rapport.

Carey was seated across from Jeff's wife, Alice, a friendly blonde in her mid-thirties. She was busy keeping her eye on their three children, and didn't bother Carey with too many personal questions. Carey was able to answer with the cover stories she'd told Ben.

Until, as Alice passed a platter of roast goose, she said, "So, how long have you and Ben been dating?"

A mouthful of corn bread caught in Carey's throat. She blinked and smiled.

"We aren't dating. I just met Ben last night. On the road. I had a car accident and he stopped to help me."

Carey carefully omitted the part about how she stayed over at Ben's house. That would only give Alice the wrong impression…again.

"Oh, that's too bad. About your accident, I mean." Alice cast her a sympathetic look, but also seemed as if she didn't quite believe that Carey and Ben were not romantically involved.

Carey could hardly blame her. She supposed to the rest of the party, they did look like a couple. They'd walked in together and were now seated side by side, with Ben's arm slung around the back of her chair in a familiar way, and he'd also just taken Lindsay into his lap so Carey could finish her dinner.

Alice's look seemed to say that maybe Carey didn't think they were involved…but they were.

One of Alice's little boys ran up to her to ask a question, interrupting the adult conversation. Carey was relieved. But suddenly she felt self-conscious. Did everyone here think she was Ben's girlfriend?

She suddenly wanted to tap the side of her glass, stand up and announce a disclaimer. "Hey, everyone…just so you know, Ben and I are not dating. We just met last night…at a car accident."

Then she felt silly. Did it matter what Ben's family thought? It would only really matter to him. After she left. He probably only saw these relatives once or twice a year anyway and most likely, didn't care what they thought about his social life.

She also knew, someplace deep inside, she was cooperating with this mistaken impression.

How easy it would be to slip into that role of his girlfriend, his romantic partner. And it was Christmas. And they were both alone. So perhaps playing this pretend game for the day was a harmless but helpful way for each of them to get through the holiday?

Ben's sister, Luanne, finally emerged, wearing kitchen whites—a chef's white jacket, and work pants. She was tall, with a full, shapely figure. She looked a few years younger than Ben and shared his good looks. Her long dark hair was pulled back in a tight ponytail and she also had the trademark Martin blue eyes, Carey noticed.

She waved as she greeted everyone, then walked around the table, dispensing kisses and handshakes to her many—now well-fed—relatives.

"Merry Christmas. Sorry I couldn't come out and join you…"

She soon reached Ben. He kissed her on the cheek. "Great meal, Lu. I'm about to burst my buttons."

Luanne patted her brother's flat stomach. "I think you're ready for the Santa costume. No pillows necessary."

Ben laughed at her teasing. He turned to Carey and introduced his sister. "Nice to meet you, Carey. I'm sorry about your accident. I heard you'll be staying over with us a few days."

Word traveled fast around here. Everyone seemed to know her story. Carey had to smile. "Yes, I am. The room is lovely…and this meal was spectacular."

"It was," Ben agreed. "A gourmet feast."

Luanne gave him an ironic look. "I think Aunt Greta had

some concerns about the goat cheese in her roasted beets, and the garlic in the mashed potatoes…but I didn't get too many complaints."

Luanne smiled and went to greet other relatives. When she was out of listening range, Ben said, "My sister is a world-class cook. She studied at the Culinary Institute and at some fancy cooking school in Paris."

Carey had gathered that. The dishes were quite sophisticated, not at all what she expected at a country inn. She wondered if Luanne worked here year-round, or had just cooked for the party.

An older man seated next to Thea rose and raised his glass. He looked polished and professional, wearing a dark blue suit and a red silk tie. Tall and lanky, he had a full head of gray hair, a long, angular face and gentle-looking brown eyes.

"A toast to the chef, Luanne Martin, who worked so hard to prepare this beautiful meal…and to her mother, Thea, our lovely hostess. Thank you both for making this such a wonderful Christmas gathering."

Everyone nodded and remarked in agreement. "Good toast, Walter! Wonderful meal…Merry Christmas…"

Carey noticed that Ben raised his glass in the toast, but remained silent. As he looked up at the older man, his expression soured.

Carey had seen Thea sitting with Walter and the way they acted toward each other during the meal. They were obviously a couple, or a least, close friends. Walter seemed comfortable enough in the family circle to make a toast, so that said something.

Thea stood up and rested her hand on Walter's shoulder.

"Thank you, Walter. That was very sweet. Thank you, all, for coming today. I know the weather made it hard for traveling. But we Maniacs are a hardy bunch. We thrive in the cold weather and snow. It's so nice for the family to be together like this on Christmas. There are some desserts coming and presents to open. And games to play. So please just relax and enjoy the day…."

Dessert and coffee were served as a buffet and the group dispersed, some remaining at the table and others wandering off to a nearby sunroom and the lobby.

Thea asked Ben to help her give out the gifts and when he took his place by the Christmas tree, Carey took the opportunity to slip away. She picked up Lindsay and headed upstairs to their room.

The baby was due for a nap and though Carey had enjoyed the party and delicious dinner more than she had expected, she had also gotten her fill of socializing and ducking personal questions.

Passing through the lobby, she passed two gray-haired women seated side by side on a settee.

"Isn't that Ben's new girlfriend?" one said. "She's cute. Look at that hair. I had hair like that when I was young."

"It's about time he started dating… How long has he been divorced now?"

The other woman answered, but Carey couldn't hear what she said.

Holding Lindsay close, she acted as if she hadn't heard a word and headed up the staircase. So there was a divorce in Ben's past. That gave her some reason why he was unattached. But why had Ben been out of the dating scene? He was so attractive. Any woman in her right mind would want to go out with him.

It was a mystery and would remain so, Carey thought. She was just passing through and it didn't make any difference to her, one way or the other. She told herself that…and tried to believe it.

Carey let herself into her room and closed the door behind her. The party sounds faded and she relished the quiet. She changed Lindsay's diaper and gave her a bottle of formula she'd fixed earlier in the day.

Lindsay quickly fell asleep after her bottle. Carey realized the portable crib was not in the room yet, so she spread a big white towel and laid her gently on her back in the middle of the bed.

She found her cell phone and dialed Paul Newton's number.

Nora, Paul's wife, answered on the second ring. She sounded happy and relieved to hear Carey's voice.

"Are you all right, dear? When we didn't hear from you, we got worried."

"I'm fine, Nora. I had a little problem with the car." Carey quickly explained the situation. "It will be in the shop a few days. I won't be getting up to Canada as quickly as I thought."

"As long as you and Lindsay are all right. Here, let me put Paul on. He's dying to talk to you...."

"Carey? What's this about a car accident?"

Carey quickly dispelled his concern. "I've been delayed a few days. But this very nice man, Ben Martin, found us and let us stay over at his house. Now I'm in a hotel in the village that his family runs, The Greenbriar Inn. I was just at their family Christmas party."

"I'm glad you weren't spending the day alone. I have some news for you. I heard something in the office on Friday, just before I left. I hung around late and sure enough, he called the investigator. It sounds like the guy has lost the trail up in Vermont. He's backtracked and started looking down in New York again."

Carey sighed. "That's good news, Paul. Thank you."

"I think you're all right for now. If I hear anything more, I'll call you, of course. And you let us know when you start off again, all right?"

"Yes, I will. Good night now. Merry Christmas."

"Merry Christmas to you, Carey. Stay safe," Paul added.

Carey said goodbye again and snapped the phone closed. A soft knock sounded on the door and she walked over to answer it.

She opened the door a crack and found Ben there, with the portable crib and all the necessary bedding.

"Oh, the crib. Come on in. Lindsay's already asleep."

"Don't worry. I'll be quiet."

Ben rolled the crib in, careful not to make a sound. He quickly set it up and Carey helped him put the sheets and blankets on.

Then she picked Lindsay up from the bed and put her down on the mattress. The baby stirred a moment, then fell asleep again.

Ben stood beside her, looking down at the baby. "She was the hit of the party."

Carey smiled. "Yes, she's very social. All the partying wore her out, though."

"How about you?" He rested his hand on her shoulder. Carey was so aware of his touch, she could hardly answer.

"It was fun. I'm glad I went after all," she admitted. "But I got a little tired, too."

His large strong hand had moved across her shoulders. "Tired of being mistaken for my girlfriend?"

The question caught her by surprise. When she turned to look at him, his eyes were lit with amusement though his expression seemed serious. He'd obviously overheard his cousin's wife, Alice, and maybe some others at the table, too.

She didn't know what to say. Then slowly she shook her head. "Actually…I didn't get tired of that at all," she confessed.

He smiled slowly, deep dimples creasing his lean cheeks. Then, before she could say another word, he leaned over and kissed her, his mouth meeting hers in a deep, hungry kiss.

He pulled her close and Carey melted in his strong embrace. He kissed her as if he'd been thinking about it all day, his mouth moving over hers, hungry, searching, tasting, testing. Savoring the taste of her.

She felt the same. She'd been thinking of being alone with him, close to him like this all day, too. Their embrace last night had been a teasing introduction, but this was the real thing.

Deeper and hotter, as if a vortex of passion had suddenly been let loose. Carey felt the power as it pulled her to the center and swallowed her whole.

Ben's hands moved over her body, slipping under her top and gliding over the thin silk camisole. Carey's hands moved over his muscular back and slipped under his shirt.

He pressed his face into the curve of her neck, his hot mouth lingering there.

"You are so beautiful, Carey…I can barely take my eyes off you…." His voice was ragged and he held her even closer. She could feel his excitement. He was ready to make love to her. She sighed and held him close, then took a step closer to the bed. His lips met hers again in a deep, soulful kiss that sent shock waves through every part of her body. Their tongues twined and twisted, teasing and tasting each other. His strong hands moved up and down her body, tracing her soft womanly curves.

Carey could never recall feeling like this, set on fire with a simple kiss. Well, the kiss hadn't been all that simple, she reflected in some distant part of her mind. Ben's kiss was masterful, confident, passionate. Sweeping aside her reservations like a tidal wave.

She wasn't sure how long they stood kissing and touching each other. Suddenly, just as Carey expected they would stretch out on the bed, the ring of a cell phone sounded, coming from Ben's back pocket.

Ben's head hung heavily on her shoulder for a moment. She couldn't tell if he was laughing…or crying. He sighed and stepped back, a self-conscious smile on his handsome face.

"I've got to take this… Sorry," he whispered. "It might be important."

Carey nodded and stepped away from him.

She felt a little like crying herself. Or at least, giving out a shriek of frustration. She hadn't been this close to a man in over a year and had gone from zero to a hundred in ten seconds flat.

She stepped over to the dresser, fumbling with the zipper on her top and feeling practically dizzy. She ran her fingers through her hair that Ben had thoroughly mussed.

She looked at herself in the mirror. Her eyes were wide and glazed looking, her mouth swollen. She looked thoroughly and completely kissed. Practically…seduced. She sighed, not sure if she was glad for the interruption, or annoyed at it.

Ben flipped his phone closed, then took a moment to smooth out his sweater and push his hair back with his hands. He glanced at her, his expression still full of longing.

"That was my pal, Harry. At the body shop. Nice of him to return a call on Christmas…but he could have had better timing. He said he's going to look at your car first thing tomorrow morning and make up an estimate. I'm working tomorrow but I can meet you there if you like."

Carey considered the offer for a moment. She was sure she could handle talking to the mechanic herself. But it wouldn't hurt to have Ben with her, she reasoned.

And that way you'll be sure to see him tomorrow, a small voice reminded her.

As if that was a good idea…

Ben suddenly seemed to have second thoughts about their embrace, too. Or was she just being silly and self-conscious? She wasn't quite sure. He stood by the door, his expression suddenly serious.

Had their unexpected explosion of passion surprised him… as much as it had surprised her?

"I guess I'd better get back to the party. People will be leaving. I need to say goodbye."

"Yes, of course." Carey nodded. "Please thank your mother again for me. I didn't get to speak to her before I left."

"I will," he promised. "See you tomorrow, then. Good night, Carey."

"Good night, Ben," she said quietly.

She watched as he opened the door and stepped out into the hall. Then she sat on the bed, and sighed.

She liked him. She liked him a lot. More than any man she'd met in a long time. Why did she have to meet a man like him right now…when her whole life was turned upside down? When she couldn't even tell him her real name?

That didn't seem fair.

But nothing seemed very fair lately.

She flopped back on the bed and folded her arms behind her head, then stared at the ceiling.

That kiss was…awesome. She still felt her body tingling, head to toe. But that was probably the start and end of it, all in one, Carey reflected.

It wouldn't be smart, or responsible, or even kind to get involved with a man like Ben. She could only end up disappointing him. Hurting him. It was going to be a struggle, but for the next few days, she had to keep him at arm's length.

Chapter Five

When Carey came down to the lobby the next morning with Lindsay, she saw Thea at the front desk, talking on the phone. Thea smiled and waved hello, then she covered the phone with her hand.

"There's breakfast in the sunroom. If you need anything for the baby, just let someone know."

Carey smiled in answer, then walked toward the sunroom, adjacent to the lobby. A row of small tables stood by the long windows. A few other guests sat eating, or reading the newspaper.

Carey found an empty table, then pulled over a high chair she spotted near the entrance. She strapped Lindsay in the seat, then checked out the buffet tables. There was a wide array of breakfast foods there, hot and cold. But she only came away with a muffin and coffee for herself, and a banana, yogurt and a mini box of Cheerios for the baby. She wasn't very hungry, but the coffee smelled good.

She had called the garage in town the first thing after waking up. It was the only station in the small village and it wasn't hard to get the phone number. The station owner, Harry Anderson, promised to look at her car the first chance he had. He mentioned that Ben had already called about the car, too, and Carey felt bad for bothering him.

There was nothing for her to do but wait. She hoped he wouldn't take too long. The news last night from Paul Newton had been some relief, but she couldn't count on private investigators looking in the wrong direction for too long.

She'd just started to feed Lindsay some yogurt when Thea walked in. "There was a call for you, Carey. From Harry Anderson. He says he's looked at your car and you should call him."

Thea set down a pink message slip with the mechanic's name and phone number. That was fast. Carey didn't think she'd hear back from him for at least a few hours.

"Mind if I sit a minute?" Thea asked.

Carey smiled. "Of course not."

Thea took a seat near Lindsay, then poured herself a cup of coffee from the silver pot a server had left on the table. The baby smiled up at her and waved her arms. Thea gave her a spoon from the table setting and Lindsay snatched it up eagerly.

"She's adorable. She looks just like you."

A frequent observation, but it always made Carey smile. "Thanks...Ben looks a lot like you."

"He has my eyes...but he mostly takes after his father. He certainly has his father's disposition. Quiet. Intelligent. Stubborn..."

"I haven't noticed Ben is especially stubborn," she replied honestly.

Thea looked surprised. "Maybe you just bring out his good side."

His lustful side seemed a more accurate description….

"I don't see how that could be. We hardly know each other," Carey pointed out.

"That doesn't have much to do with it, dear." Thea smiled in a knowing way. "How was the room? Were you comfortable last night?"

"Very comfortable. It was perfect." The suite had to be one of the best rooms in the hotel. Carey wondered about the rate. Thea hadn't mentioned it and in their rushed arrival yesterday, no one had even asked her to check in and register.

Which was fine with Carey, since she was traveling under an assumed name, and using a fake ID that Paul had helped her purchase. She preferred to show it as little as possible.

But she wasn't sure she could really afford the hotel room. She had a small nest egg, some savings she'd scraped together from her salary and a loan from Paul and Nora. She had to be very careful with her money.

"It has a beautiful view," Carey added. "It must be one of your best rooms. Most expensive, I mean."

Thea sipped her coffee and glanced at Carey over the rim of her cup. "Don't worry about it. If we need that particular suite for some reason, I'll just move you to another. We don't get many guests between Christmas and New Year's. The room would just be sitting empty."

Was Thea offering Carey the room for free? Carey couldn't quite believe her generosity.

"But I can't just stay here without paying you anything…"

"Of course you can," Thea insisted in a pleasant but firm tone. "People do it all the time. All of our friends and family. Besides, your car repairs are going to be very costly, from what Ben told me. You have enough to worry about. I wouldn't feel right charging you under the circumstances. Honestly."

Carey guessed that Ben had told his mother all about her.

As much as he knew. That she was a widow and needed a job. And obviously, didn't have much money.

"Did Ben ask you to do this for me?"

Thea smiled and lifted her chin. "I think he ought to answer that himself. Let's just say, once I heard about your situation, I wouldn't have it otherwise."

"Thank you," Carey said sincerely. "It's very considerate. You don't even know me…" Her voice trailed off. She didn't know what else to say.

"I know what it's like to lose your husband. And you're awfully young besides…" Thea reached over and patted her hand. "I have to get back to work. Let me know if you need anything."

Carey watched the older woman leave the room, checking the table settings and straightening out a few items on the buffet tables as she swept past.

These past few months, escaping from Quinn, Carey had been forced to face the darker side of human nature. Thea reminded her that people could reach out with kindness, too. She would have to figure out some way to repay Ben's mother for her hospitality. And Ben. She was sure he was behind it all. But thanking him had become a problem. Her feelings for him were mixed with something more than gratitude. Something she didn't dare encourage.

Lindsay seemed content in her high chair, playing with the spoon Thea had given her, preferring it even to the plastic toys Carey had pulled out of the baby bag.

Carey took out her cell phone and dialed the garage. Harry Anderson, the owner, answered on the first ring.

"This is Carey Mooreland. I got a message that you've looked at my car?"

"Oh…right. Miss Mooreland… Listen, I know you're anxious for the estimate and I promised Ben I'd do it real quick for you. But I took a quick look at the damage and I thought you should know, it's going to be tough to find some of those parts.

The car is pretty old and there's only one dealer around here who's going to carry any of this stuff. Or even know where to find it. Sometimes I can call around and find used parts that are still in good condition. It will save you some, too. I just need time to check it all out for you."

Carey's spirits sank. She had expected better news. "How long do you think that it will take?"

"Gee, hard to say. At least till the end of the day. Maybe even tomorrow."

"I see." Carey sighed. She felt so frustrated. But she didn't have any choice. "Well, all right then. I guess it can't be helped. I'll just wait to hear from you, Mr. Anderson."

Carey gave him her cell phone number, so he could call directly, then said goodbye and hung up.

This was not a good sign. If it took two days just to get an estimate on the repair, how long would it take to actually fix the car?

But she couldn't blame the messenger for the bad news. The car *was* old. She was surprised the mechanic hadn't advised her just to junk it. Most people probably would have. Unfortunately, she didn't have that option.

She wondered if she should just leave the car and keep going. Maybe rent a car or find a bus that would take her up to Canada? But that seemed impractical, too. She'd still need a car once she got there. Paul had told her she was safe in Maine. So far, anyway.

Carey pushed back the wave of fear that always seemed to be hovering on the edge of her mind, threatening to overwhelm her. She wasn't sure what to do with herself while she waited for more news from the garage. If she hung around the hotel the whole day, all she'd think about was the men who were trying to find her…and wondering when she'd see Ben again.

Neither were very productive preoccupations.

She rose and picked up Lindsay out of the high chair, then

picked up the baby bag. Sunlight streamed through the row of long windows. The day was clear with a brilliant blue sky. A walk in town might do her good, she thought. She could use the fresh air and needed some supplies for Lindsay—diapers, wipes and more baby food.

Up in their room, she dressed them both in warm clothes, then fitted Lindsay's baby carrier over her shoulders and slipped the baby in the pouch.

Lindsay loved to ride in it, Carey knew, and a stroll in the cold air was a sure way to tire her out for a morning nap.

As she passed through the lobby, Thea waved from the front desk. "Taking a walk?"

Carey nodded. "I need a few things for Lindsay."

"There's a discount drugstore on Willow Street. Don't go to the first one, near the bank. Very overpriced."

Carey appreciated the tip. "Okay, thanks."

"Could you do me a small favor while you're out?" Thea leaned closer and held out a cartridge from a computer printer. "I'm trying to send out some new brochures and the printer ran out of ink. There's a stationery store in town that stocks these. Just down Main Street, across from the diner. We have an account. Just say you're from the inn…"

"Sure. No problem." Carey took the cartridge, which was wrapped in a plastic bag and also had a little note inside, with the brand and style number written on it.

"Is there anything else you need there?"

Thea hesitated. "Well…if you don't mind. There are a few things we could use for the office."

She made Carey a quick list. "I don't want you to carry too much. Please watch your step in the snow. Do you think the baby will be warm enough?"

Carey smiled at her concern. "She's fine. She loves riding in this thing."

"She certainly looks cute in it." Thea tickled Lindsay under her chin and made the baby laugh and wave her arms and legs in the holder, as if she were trying to fly.

Thea laughed and looked eager to play with the baby more when suddenly, two red buttons on the old-fashioned telephone lit up at once.

"I need to get that. Thanks again, dear." She reached for the phone and hit a button, the pitch of her voice changing instantly to a smooth, professional tone.

"Greenbriar Inn. Can I help you…?"

Carey left the inn, glad to have a destination. She wondered if there was some other way she might help Thea while she waited for her car. Ben had mentioned that the hotel staff had been streamlined. There didn't seem to be anyone else working at the front desk or in the office. She certainly looked as if she could use some help there.

It was chilly outside, but there was no wind and the bright sun shone down, reflecting off the newly fallen snow, making everything look clean and new.

She walked along the green, then turned up Main Street. Most of the shops were open and the sidewalks shoveled clear of snow. Carey enjoyed taking her time and looking in the store windows.

The buildings were quaint and old-fashioned, but well kept. The town reminded her a bit of Blue Lake, Vermont, where she'd been so content and peaceful for such a short time. She had the urge to call her friends there, Rachel and Julia, just to let them know she was all right.

No, it wasn't a good idea. She might let her guard down and give her friends a clue to her real whereabouts. She couldn't risk it. Maybe once she was safely up in Canada, where it would be harder for Quinn to find her.

Carey wandered down Main Street. She stopped at a café

and bought a hot chocolate. Then found the drugstore on Willow Street and bought the things Lindsay needed.

Heading farther down the main avenue, she passed the Village Hall. A sign on the adjacent building said Police Station.

Was Ben in there, working? It was hard to picture him sitting at a desk, even for a short time. He was probably out in his cruiser, giving out speeding tickets or saving people from snowstorms, or whatever it was he did all day. She wondered what time he finished work and if he'd stop at the hotel on his way home.

He had not been far from her thoughts all morning. She hadn't felt like this about a man in a long time and it was confusing and annoying and exciting, all at the same time.

She kept thinking about the way he'd kissed her and touched her. The way she'd kissed him back. Their response to each other had been so powerful, so honest and uninhibited….

She wondered if it had been too much for him. Maybe he'd been scared by his own feelings. Some men were like that. They came on strong, then ran for cover. She felt a bit scared of her own response to him, as well. Maybe *scared* was not the right word. She was more…surprised. And awestruck.

But if he'd cooled off about her now, maybe that was just as well, Carey decided.

She headed back down the opposite side of the street and found the stationery store. A helpful clerk located the correct ink cartridge and the other supplies on Thea's list. The bag wasn't very heavy, though Carey was starting to feel Lindsay's weight in the baby carrier, pulling on her neck and shoulders as she headed back to the inn.

She heard a car horn sound right beside her and she jumped. She turned to see a police cruiser. Her breath caught in her throat. Had someone finally caught up with her? The district attorney's office in Cleveland… Had they put out a search for her?

Then she realized it was Ben. She was glad to see him. More

than she dared to show. She almost felt as if her longing thoughts had summoned him.

He rolled down the window on the street side and called out to her. "I thought that was you. Out sightseeing?"

"I needed a few things for Lindsay and Thea asked me to stop by the stationery store for her."

"Hop in. I'll give you a lift. I have Lindsay's car seat with me. I left it in the back of the SUV yesterday. I was just about to drop it at the inn."

Without waiting for her answer, he hopped out of the car and helped her put the packages in the back and Lindsay in her seat.

Carey got in the cruiser and sat in the front seat, beside him. The car felt close and intimate, reminding her of Christmas Eve night and driving back to his house in the snowstorm.

"So, how do you like Greenbriar?"

"It's very pretty. I'm not surprised you came back here to live."

"You aren't?" He glanced at her with a wry smile. "Sometimes I am."

Carey didn't answer right away. She glanced out the window, watching the storefronts pass by. "I spoke to Harry Anderson this morning. The estimate on my car is going to take longer than usual. He said it's old and it will be hard to find some parts."

Ben nodded. "I know. I stopped by to see him a few minutes ago."

She turned to face him. "You didn't need to do that. I can handle it."

Ben shrugged. "I'm sure you can. I just want to help you. It's a small town and he's a friend. It helps around here to know people."

"I guess so," she agreed, though her tone was reluctant.

He glanced at her. "I think you've been taking care of yourself and Lindsay for so long, it's hard for you to let anyone help you."

She glanced at him, but didn't answer. She knew what he

said was true. But he wasn't just anyone. She knew the more he helped, the more grateful she'd feel…and the more guilty, for deceiving him. And the more she would care about him.

She didn't want to have feelings for him. More feelings, she silently amended. Even though it seemed illogical and impossible, and even though they'd only known each other for a few days, she already did.

But all of this was impossible to explain. Even if she was free to give him an honest answer.

"You're right. I'm not used to it. Even when Tom was alive, he wasn't…that type of guy." She stared straight ahead, not daring to look at him.

"Really? What type of guy was he?" Ben's tone was relaxed and conversational, but she still sensed his interest.

"Tom was…very charming. Social. He liked to enjoy himself, see his friends. He didn't like to worry about what he called 'the fine print in life.'"

"Like paying the bills, that sort of thing?" Ben asked.

Carey nodded. "He pretty much left the annoying details to me."

She was used to doing everything herself. Even when she was married to Tom, she took care of all the household obligations, paying the bills, finding repairmen or fixing things herself to save money.

"I get the picture." Ben sounded almost angry, imagining her marriage.

Carey didn't answer right away.

"Tom wasn't a bad person," she said finally. "Just…immature. We got married impulsively, I guess, and we weren't very happy," she admitted. "When I got pregnant, we decided to try to stay together and make things work. But I'm not sure the marriage would have lasted if… Well, it might not have lasted after all," she said finally.

They had reached the inn. Ben pulled up in front and parked. He turned off the engine and looked over at her.

"I'm sorry I spoke harshly about your late husband. I apologize. I had no right."

Ben seemed to care about her. Maybe that gave him the right, Carey thought, though she didn't share the insight with him.

"It's okay. I don't like to talk about the past much."

"Me, either." Ben spoke quietly. He glanced at her, then got out of the car.

He took the packages from the back. Carey got out on her side and retrieved Lindsay, then followed Ben up the steps into the hotel.

She would have liked a chance to ask Ben about the marriage in his past, but for one thing, he'd never mentioned it. She'd only overheard the information. And for another, his last comment seemed to warn her off that topic. Now that they were going inside the opportunity had passed.

They walked into the lobby and Thea was just coming down the stairway with an armful of folded towels. She set them on the front desk, then walked quickly to meet Carey.

"Here, let me help you with those bags." Thea took both of the shopping bags from Ben.

"Ben saw me walking back and gave me a ride."

"My, what a coincidence." Thea's dry tone and slight smile made Carey feel embarrassed. She noticed Ben practically blush.

"I was on my way over to bring back the car seat," he explained. "I'll go get it before I forget again."

"Yes, good idea." Carey turned her attention back to Thea. "That yellow bag from the drugstore is mine."

"Oh yes, of course." Thea handed the bag back, then peered inside the one from the stationery store. "You got the ink thingy. Good. It's such a bother to change. I'd better wait until tonight, when I have more time. Or maybe I'll call Walter."

She had to call her friend Walter to change an ink cartridge? Poor Thea. She was definitely technologically challenged.

"I can do it for you," Carey offered.

"Oh…don't worry. I don't want to put you to any more trouble. I'll have Walter do it. Next time he comes over."

"No, really. Let me. It only takes a minute."

Thea gave her a doubtful look. "I don't want to keep you from the baby, Carey. She must need a nap or a bottle or something."

"She'll be fine for a minute or two. You can hold her for me. Where's the printer? Back here?"

She knew Thea was just trying to be polite. She didn't want Carey to feel obliged, as if she had to help out because she was getting a free room. But Carey was eager—and determined— to pay her back in some small way if she could.

Carey walked around to the back of the desk and then headed to the small office.

Thea trotted behind her. "The printer is on the table near the window. I've been having trouble getting the brochures to come out straight on the page," she confessed. "Maybe you could show me what I'm doing wrong…."

A few minutes later, the new ink cartridge was in place and Carey sat at the computer, putting some final touches on the new brochure.

Thea had made a good start, but Carey could see that with a few small changes, the copy would be easier to read and also fit the pages better.

Thea held Lindsay and amused her, in between answering the telephone and sorting out mail. "That looks marvelous. So much better," she kept saying as she glanced over Carey's shoulder.

Ben poked his head in the doorway. "What are you doing in here? I thought you went up to your room."

"I'm just helping with the new brochure."

"That's nice of you. Computers are not her strong point," he said diplomatically.

Thea gave him a look. "If I was *completely* perfect, I'd be very boring."

"Yes, Mother. So you often remind us… I've got to get back to work. I left the car seat in the lobby."

"Oh, bring it in here, will you?" Carey glanced at him over her shoulder. "It pushes back into a cradle position. Lindsay can sleep in it while I work."

"Excellent idea. Not that I don't love holding her," Thea said. "But she might be more comfortable."

The baby was nestled on her shoulder, her eyes half-closed already. Carey was surprised. Lindsay was normally tense with strangers and would barely tolerate anyone holding her, especially if Carey was in view. But Thea seemed to have a way with babies. Especially this one.

Ben returned a moment later with the car seat, which he set on the floor near Carey's desk. Thea carefully handed the baby to Carey, then walked out to the front, where a guest had sounded the desk bell. "Be right back," she whispered.

Carey pushed the seat back to the right position and gently put Lindsay down. There was a blanket folded on the cushions and she opened it up and spread it over the baby.

"Do you think she's warm enough? I can find another blanket somewhere," Ben said.

Carey stood by Ben and gazed down at the baby. "She'll be okay. She has on layers of heavy clothes."

"If you say so. Well, I'd better get going."

He turned to her. She hadn't realized that they were standing so close together, her shoulder brushing his arm.

Their eyes met for a long moment and she noticed his gaze wander down to her mouth. She couldn't help but recall the way he'd kissed her and wondered if he was thinking about it again, too.

If he was thinking of kissing her now…

He took a deep breath and stepped back toward the door. "I'll see you," he said quietly.

Soon, I hope, she wanted to say.

Instead, she nodded. "Thanks for the ride."

"I'm getting used to driving you around. Maybe I should quit my job and become your private chauffeur. You won't need to have your car fixed."

Carey smiled but didn't answer. If only that were true. She did need her car to keep running. Far away from here.

When he'd finally disappeared from view, she turned back to the computer screen. But she couldn't help overhearing Ben talking to Thea just outside the door.

"Do you want to come back tonight for dinner?" Thea asked. "We'll wait for you."

"I've got a long shift. I won't be off until ten," Carey heard him answer.

Carey felt disappointed. She'd thought she might get to see him again later. She sighed, annoyed at herself. It was just as well.

Every minute in Ben's company, her feelings for him grew more complicated. And made her life even more difficult. As if it wasn't hard enough.

Lindsay slept soundly while Carey worked on the computer. She guessed the entire process was a puzzle for Thea. She was no tech genius herself, but she'd done a lot of office work and a project like this was easy for her. She was glad for the chance to return Thea's generosity.

Thea was mainly occupied out front and finally, Carey printed out a draft copy and showed her the changes.

Carey could tell by her expression as she read it through that she was very pleased and impressed.

"This is wonderful. Do you do this type of work professionally?"

Carey shook her head, nearly laughing. "It's just some simple graphics. I took the sketch of the inn from your letterhead and scanned that in, on top. Then fiddled with the copy and the type. I've had a lot of office jobs. You pick up computer skills here and there."

"You're being too modest, dear. It's very artistic. I would have paid someone a fortune to make up something this nice."

"You had a good start," she said honestly. "How many copies do you need? Lindsay is still asleep. I can run them off right now."

"Would you? If I just get near that darn machine, it starts flashing all kinds of annoying messages. I can never get it to work right."

They decided to start with two hundred copies. Thea watched as Carey loaded the printer with special paper and started the print job.

"How will you send these out? Do you have a mailing list?" Carey asked.

Thea seemed puzzled by the question. "Of course I do. People who have stayed here. Or who call for information."

"I mean, in the computer. To print out the envelopes?"

"The computer will do that for you?"

Carey struggled to hide her amusement. "If there's a list of names and addresses typed in, yes, it will do that pretty easily. It's called mail merge."

"Mail merge. Yes, I think I've heard of that…but I've never had the time to figure it out," Thea said. "Most of the addresses are in there. Somewhere…" She glanced at Carey. "Would it be too much trouble for you to show me how? Not right now. Tomorrow, maybe. If you have some time free?"

"All my time is free, Thea. Until the car is ready."

Thea's expression relaxed to her usual, warm smile. "I know it's very selfish of me, but I hope Harry takes a long time with those repairs... Not just because you're so clever with the computer, either."

She patted Carey's shoulder then headed out to the front desk again.

Carey felt touched by the compliment. A small but insistent voice warned her to keep her distance from everyone in this place. Not just Ben, but Thea and everyone at the inn. That would be the smart thing to do.

But it was hard for Carey to remain distant and cool toward people who treated her so warmly. She could help Thea out, for a few days, Carey reasoned. It was the right thing to do.

Even if she did feel herself getting more and more involved here.

Chapter Six

"Miss Mooreland? Harry Anderson. At the garage?"

"Yes, Mr. Anderson. I know who you are." Carey balanced the cell phone between her cheek and shoulder. She'd just gotten out of bed and was in the middle of changing Lindsay. "Any news about my car?"

Harry Anderson had a lot of news. None of it was good and all of it sounded expensive. First he described everything that needed to be fixed or replaced, half of which she didn't understand.

Carey said, "Uh-huh…uh-huh…" at each opportunity. "How long do you think it will take to fix it?" she finally cut in.

"Let's see, today's Thursday. If I can get all the parts in here by Saturday, we should be done by Monday night. But that's New Year's Eve. So if we don't finish up, were looking at Wednesday, the second. I can bang out the hood. But that's not including a paint job and the ding in the fender."

"I don't care what it looks like," she said honestly. "I just need to get back on the road."

"I understand. We'll take care of it as quick as we can," he promised.

She could have had the car towed to another garage, on the highway or in a different town. But she didn't think they would fix it any faster and it would definitely cost more, after the towing. Ben had told her Harry Anderson wouldn't cheat her and she felt that was true.

When Carey hung up, she started to worry. She wasn't sure if it was safe to stay in Greenbriar for four more days. She decided to call Paul, to see if he'd heard anything more about Quinn's investigators, or any news from the district attorney's office.

"Hello, Sunny. Where are you?" She could tell by the tone of his voice—and by the fact that he'd used his special name for her—that he was at work and not alone, so couldn't speak freely.

"I'm still in Greenbriar. I just heard that my car won't be ready until Monday."

"That's not so bad. Listen, those friends of ours, down in New York? Looks like they're going to stay longer. Still sightseeing."

"Quinn's investigators are still looking for me in New York?" she asked him, wanting to make sure she had understood him.

"That's right. I just heard this morning. It's a big city. Sounds like they'll be there for a while."

"What about the D.A.'s office? Do they still think I helped Quinn? Are they still looking for me?"

"Hard to say. I'll try to find out more for you. It's been very quiet over there. The quiet before the storm, maybe."

"I hope not, Paul. I would love to help put Quinn behind bars. You know I would. But I can't risk it."

"I understand. Believe me…"

A knock sounded on the door, startling her. "Hold on a second. There's someone here."

She held the phone aside and answered the door. It was Ben. Dressed in blue jeans and a gray V-neck sweater with a white T-shirt underneath. His dark hair was still damp from a shower, his cheeks smoothly shaven. The unexpected sight of him jolted her senses, the kick stronger than a giant cup of coffee.

"Ben…what are you doing here?"

"Well, good morning to you, too." His blue eyes swept over her, darkening in a way that made her remember she was still wearing her robe and nightgown. Her hand moved up to the top of her robe, pulling closed the gaping opening.

"Did I interrupt you? I can come back later."

She stared down at the phone in her hand. She wondered how long he'd been standing out there. Had he overheard any of her conversation? She didn't think he'd purposely try to eavesdrop, but sometimes it just happened by accident.

She quickly lifted the phone to her ear. "Paul? Sorry, someone is here. I have to go."

"Okay, pal. Good to hear from you. I'll be in touch if I have news. Stay safe."

"Same to you," she said quietly, then snapped the phone shut. She could feel Ben watching her. She had the feeling he was curious to know who she'd been speaking with.

"I was just catching up with a friend," she said. "Nothing important."

"Your friend in Portland?"

Portland? She didn't know what he meant for a moment.

Then she remembered her story. It was getting harder to keep track of her lies. Or maybe just harder to keep lying to him.

"Um…no. Someone else," she said quickly.

"I need to fix a few things in this room today." He held up a long list on a sheet of yellow paper. "Room 23, door sticks.

Light switch in big closet. Doorknob to balcony jiggles…" He looked up at her. "Can I take a look at the light switch and see what part I need?"

"Sure, come in. Lindsay is awake. She's just playing in her crib."

He followed her into the room and the heavy door closed with a snapping sound.

Carey felt suddenly aware of having on just a nightgown and thin robe. Aware of the big, wide bed, the sheets and blankets already in a tangle.

Aware of how good he looked this morning, standing barely more than an arm's length away from her. She could smell the soap on his skin and a hint of spicy aftershave. His hard, masculine body was outlined in the dark sweater and jeans. His shoulders were broad, his waist slim. His long, lean legs seemed to go on forever.

He had removed the cover from the switch outside the closet and was peering inside with a small flashlight. Then he pushed up his sleeves, displaying muscular forearms covered with dark hair.

Carey knew she should stop looking at him, but couldn't help herself. Her thoughts scattered, distracted by being alone with him.

"So…is this your day off?" she asked, searching for conversation.

"A day off from the police force. There's always plenty to catch up on here."

Good. That means he'll be around all day, she thought.

"It's a big place," she said.

"And old. And needs to be totally renovated," he added. He'd taken out a small screwdriver and was removing something in the switch box.

She leaned back against the wall, watching him work.

"I guess that would cost a lot of money."

"A whole lot. And business isn't going that well. Of course, if you don't keep things up, it will go even worse. It's a catch-22."

"Yes, I can see that." From the little she'd seen yesterday in Thea's office, running an inn was far more complicated than she'd ever imagined.

He glanced at her, his gaze sweeping down her body, making her suddenly conscious again of her lack of apparel. She tightened the belt on her robe and crossed her arms over her chest.

"Any news about your car?" he asked.

"I just spoke with Harry Anderson. He thinks it might be done by Monday."

"New Year's Eve?"

Carey nodded. "That's right."

"So you'll be leaving in…four days."

"Probably."

She tried to figure out his reaction to this news. His face was without expression, his eyes focused on the wall switch.

"That's not too long."

"No, not long at all. It will go by quickly," she added.

"Yes, it will," he said without looking up at her.

She realized she may have sounded happy about leaving. When in fact, she had mixed feelings.

Part of her wanted to pack up and run off today. Another part wanted to stay. The part that wanted to stay seemed totally in possession of her at that moment. She felt a wave of longing as she watched Ben put the switch plate cover back in place. She would miss him. She felt as if she already did.

She heard something drop and then roll on the carpet. It sounded like a piece from the switch cover. She saw the screw land near her feet and quickly bent to pick it up.

When she stood up, he was standing very close. Face-to-face. He stared into her eyes a moment, then his gaze slid lower, sliding down her body in a way that sent a coil of heat from head to toe. Her mouth went dry. She licked her lips before she could speak and saw him react to that tiny gesture.

"I think you forgot something."

He didn't answer. Just stared down at her. She felt his breath on her bare skin and the heat of his body, close to her.

"I did?" he asked quietly. He looked as muddled and full of longing as she felt. Maybe even more so.

"Don't you need this?" She held out the screw from the switch plate. "I found it on the floor."

"Oh…right. Sure."

She handed it to him, dropping it in his opened, flat palm. He nodded, without looking up at her. Then stepped back slowly, as if he'd been standing at the edge of a cliff, about to fall off.

He slipped the screw in his pocket, picked up his toolbox and walked to the door. His handsome face wore a grim, resigned expression, his square jaw locked in place.

"I think you forgot something, too," he said finally.

She looked at him curiously.

Before she could ask what he meant, he said, "I think you ought to put some clothes on, Carey."

Then he turned and disappeared out the door. Carey stood in the middle of the room, clutching the two sides of her robe together.

She swallowed hard. She needed to shower and dress and start her day. A *cold* shower would be a good idea.

Four more days. Could she keep out of his way for that long? Did she really even want to?

Carey's morning passed much the same as the day before. She ate breakfast in the sunroom and then decided a walk into town again would be a good idea. Lindsay needed the fresh air and Carey knew she didn't need to be hanging around the inn, waiting to run into Ben again.

She took her time, walking into shops she hadn't explored the day before and even visiting the library. In the periodical room she found a recent copy of the *Cleveland Tribune*. She flipped through, feeling a pang of nostalgia for her hometown. Then in the business section, she saw a small article about Quinn's legal troubles. Construction Company Defrauds Banks of Millions—Investigation Widens.

Her heart raced and she abruptly sat down. She held the newspaper closer to read the article, but her vision blurred. She felt for a moment as if she might faint. Then took a few deep, calming breaths. She looked around the reading room. No one seemed to have noticed her distress. Except for a librarian sitting at the reference desk, across from Carey's chair.

She peered at Carey over the edge of her reading glasses. "Are you all right, miss?"

Carey forced a smile. "I'm fine. A little warm in here." She pulled her scarf loose and zipped open her parka.

The librarian seemed satisfied and went back to her work.

Carey returned to the news article, scanning it quickly. Peerless Construction, Quinn's company, was mentioned in the second paragraph. Quinn McCauley was mentioned by name soon after.

It sounded as if there wasn't enough evidence yet to charge Quinn with a crime. She knew he was clever and adept at covering his tracks. But she also knew he had been greedy and made some mistakes. It sounded as if he would get caught, sooner or later, she thought. And it could not be too soon for her.

A line toward the end of the article caught her attention. "The investigation is ongoing. Others may be indicted soon and subpoenaed to testify should the case go to trial."

"Others." That was her.

Well, she couldn't take part in a trial if no one could find her. They'll have to start without me, Carey thought, swallowing back a lump of fear.

She returned the newspaper to the rack, bundled up Lindsay and they left the library.

When she returned to the inn, Thea was at the reception desk, sorting out the mail. She looked up from her task and smiled. "Did you two have a good walk?"

"Very good. I think the cold air made Lindsay sleepy. I can work on the brochures again, Thea. As soon as Lindsay goes down for her nap," Carey offered.

Thea glanced at her. Carey could tell she was pleased, but unsure if she should accept the offer. "I appreciate your help, Carey. But I really don't want you to feel obligated."

"I don't feel obligated, Thea. More like...bored?" Thea looked up again. Carey caught her eye. "I'm not good at sitting around, gazing at the scenery. Or even reading a book. I'm used to being busy. I'll get a little nutty if I don't have anything to do."

"A little nutty, huh? Well, you'll fit right in with this family," Thea muttered under her breath. She swiped up a stack of envelopes and slipped a rubber band around the middle. "If you really want to help, I have a special assignment today. The brochures can wait a bit. Come with me..."

Thea crooked her finger in an enticing gesture and Carey followed. They walked through the dining room, then through the big swinging doors that led to the kitchen.

Carey had worked in restaurants and the sight of a commercial kitchen was not unknown to her, though she always found it a very interesting place to be.

The kitchen at Greenbriar Inn was medium size, with old-looking fixtures, though everything was sparkling clean. The walls were all white tile and the floor, dark red. A long chrome worktable ran down the middle of the room, dividing it in half.

A huge cast-iron stove, wall ovens and a double-layered grill took up one half of the room, flanked by a deep chrome sink. She also saw shelves of glasses and dishes, along with a refrigerator with a sliding glass door.

There was only one kitchen worker present, a young man in whites, stirring yellow batter in a huge aluminum bowl. Carey saw Luanne at the far end of the room. She seemed to be examining the contents of a cardboard box and when Thea and Carey reached her, she had pulled out a large pineapple. Carey could see the box was filled with fruit and guessed that Luanne was checking a delivery.

"Look at this. It's a beauty, right? Not bad for late December," Luanne said. "I knew that new produce place would be worth it."

"I'm sure it was expensive," Thea said.

"It wasn't cheap…but I need it for a sorbet." Luanne placed it back in the box and brushed her hand on her apron. "You can get away with some canned, but you need the real deal for presentation."

Thea glanced at Carey. "My daughter knows a lot about presentation. She could put anything on a plate and make it look appetizing. Even an old shoe, for goodness' sake."

Luanne glanced at Carey. "I've upgraded the entrées. We hardly ever serve old shoes here anymore."

Carey smiled at her tart tone.

"Speaking of our upgraded entrées," Thea cut in, "I wanted to show Carey the new menu. She did wonders with the brochure yesterday. I'm sure she can help us improve the menu layout."

Luanne cast Carey a curious glance. "Okay, let's see what you think."

Luanne walked over to a metal desk in an alcove near the door. She leafed through some papers and returned with a manila folder. Carey was holding Lindsay and shifted the baby to her other side in order to see the sheets Luanne held out to her.

She looked the pages over slowly. She felt put on the spot.

She didn't want to hurt anyone's feelings. "I don't have all that much experience with layouts and graphic design. I just know some of the basics…"

"She's just being modest," Thea said to Luanne. "She's really very good." Then to Carey, she added, "We're trying to market the dining room as a restaurant. Not just for guests staying here. We want to do some advertising, maybe even change the name of the room to something…"

"Less stuffy and old-fashioned. Right now it sounds like, Ye Olde Stuffed Baked Potato." Luanne's tone was flat and wry.

Carey couldn't help smiling, but she could tell Thea was a bit miffed by the joke.

"I'm glad you told me that," Carey said. "I was thinking that the type could be changed to something a little cleaner looking. More…modern. It is hard to read this curly script."

Luanne looked at her mother. "Okay. Point taken," Thea said. "That was Walter's idea. I did think it looked too much like the old menu."

"Go on," Luanne coaxed Carey. "What else do you think?"

Carey took a breath. This one was a little harder.

"Well…there's a lot of description about the food here. It's a lot to read. Probably too much. Some of it is helpful…but I feel as if I've had a meal just reading through appetizers."

"I agree." Now it was Thea's turn to look at Luanne. "We don't need to give the whole recipe. Just the highlights."

Luanne crossed her arms over her chest and frowned. "All right. Enough said. Can you edit it down a little for us, Carey?"

Carey shrugged. "Okay. Do you have a minute? It will probably go faster if we work together. I don't want to leave out anything important."

"Heaven forbid we forget to mention a shiitake mushroom, here or there," Thea quipped.

Luanne gave her mother a look.

Carey would have laughed but she was distracted by Lindsay, who had grown fretful. Carey bounced her in her arms.

"I think she's ready for a bottle and a nap," Thea said.

"Do you have a bottle handy? I'll heat it for you," Luanne offered.

"Yes, I do. Right in my purse. I brought one into town, just in case."

Luanne took out the plastic bottle, filled it with milk and warmed it in a pot of hot water she poured from a spigot on the coffeemaker.

Thea and Luanne watched as Lindsay eagerly drank. "It's lovely to have a baby around," Thea said with a sigh. "They're so sweet and innocent. They bring such joy."

She glanced at her daughter. "I wish you and your brother would get to work on some grandchildren. I'm not getting any younger. I'd like to have some energy to play...and do things with them."

Luanne rolled her eyes. "I think you have plenty of energy, Mom. That's not the problem."

"Oh...? There's a problem?" Thea's eyes widened.

Carey had been patting Lindsay's back and she suddenly drew everyone's attention with a giant burp.

"Whoa, that was a winner," Luanne said.

"It's healthy to get the extra air up. Children get stomach-aches otherwise," Thea said. She gazed down at Lindsay and put her arms out. "May I hold her now?"

Carey handed the baby up to her. "Sure... She's going to fall asleep on you, though."

"That's what I was hoping," Thea said quietly.

She hugged the baby to her shoulder and sort of waltzed around the room, humming a little song. Carey knew Lindsay would be out in no time.

The car seat was still in Thea's office. Carey brought it back to the kitchen so Lindsay could nap in her sight while she and Luanne reviewed the menu.

Thea set the baby down gently, then returned to her own work. Carey and Luanne were left alone to rewrite the food descriptions.

The list of appetizers went quickly. Then they did the entrées and salads. There was one with blue cheese, grilled chicken, dried cranberries and toasted pecans. The description made Carey's mouth water.

"Mmm…that sounds yummy," Carey said.

"Hungry? We can do some taste testing, too. That will be helpful. Besides, you must be ready for lunch."

She was hungry. It was past one. They worked some more while Luanne made them each a salad. By the time she sat down again and served the food, they were halfway done with editing the menu.

"Roughage break," Luanne announced. "More dressing?"

Carey shook her head. "It's just right."

"I hope my mother isn't driving you crazy," Luanne said between mouthfuls. "She can be…intense."

Carey could see that. But she genuinely liked Thea.

"She's been very generous to let us stay here while the car is being repaired. I just want to return the favor."

"Don't worry, she loves having you here." Luanne waved her hand. "She wasn't kidding when she said she wants grandchildren. She drives us crazy. She was pretty disappointed when Ben got divorced. Not that she liked his ex-wife all that much. But there went her best chance for babies in the family."

"Ben didn't tell me he was married. But I did hear a remark at the Christmas party," she admitted. She hoped Luanne would tell her more, but she didn't want to seem too nosy.

"He doesn't like to talk about it. They were living down in North Carolina. That's where they met. At school. Eva was…difficult. I never got along with her," Luanne admitted. "She was the real fussy type. Nothing ever seemed good enough."

Carey had guessed as much, but it was interesting to hear it confirmed.

"She didn't like the idea of Ben being in law enforcement. That was one problem."

"She was worried about him? I mean, being in danger, getting shot at or something?"

Carey knew she would worry about all those things if the man she loved was in law enforcement. It seemed very tame here, in this picturesque place, but she knew for a fact there were dangerous people everywhere.

"I don't think that was it," Luanne said with a small smile. "She never said as much. She was worried that Ben would never make that much money. Even though he was doing something he loved and they lived very comfortably."

Luanne paused and buttered a piece of warm sourdough bread she'd served with the salad. "That was probably why she left him. She met someone else. A lawyer, I think. She started the affair while Ben was up here, visiting my dad. After he'd been diagnosed. It was a blow for my brother. A blow to his pride and…it's made it hard for him to get close to anyone new. He really loved her. And trusted her."

Carey nodded. "I understand."

She felt a dull pain in her heart. Sympathy for Ben and also the pain of her own deception. This story alone should remind her that Ben was off-limits. He'd been hurt by a woman who had deceived him. If they got involved, Carey knew she would be deceiving him, too. She was already, she realized.

"He hasn't met anyone he really likes since. Not that we've ever heard," Luanne added with a shrug. "Please don't let him know I told you all this, okay? He'll never forgive me."

"Don't worry, I won't." Carey took a bite of her salad. She

was eager to learn more about Ben, but thought it was better to change the subject.

"How about you, Luanne? What's it like being a single woman up here?"

Luanne laughed. "It's hell frozen over. I wake up every day and thank heaven above I already have a boyfriend. He's working in Portland, at a new restaurant on the waterfront. The whole area down there has been renovated. It's very hot. We don't get to see each other much. But when we do it's just… really great."

She nodded and smiled. Carey could tell from the light in her eyes and the blush on her cheeks that she was in love.

Carey felt a twinge of envy. Luanne was lucky. She'd found someone to love and the timing was right. She wished Luanne well. She was a dear, funny, bright woman and any guy would be lucky to catch her.

"What's his name?" Carey asked. "Where did you meet? How long have you known each other? I want all the details, please."

Luanne sighed and rolled her eyes. "We met at cooking school. We always liked each other, but we didn't go out right away. We were in some of the same classes and liked to cook together. When we graduated, we went our separate ways. I came back here and after a while, he got the job in Portland. So he called me. We met, just to say hello. And that was that." Luanne grinned. "By the time we picked a dessert to share, we just…knew."

"What a nice story," Carey said finally. It gave her hope. Good things could happen, too. To anyone.

"How romantic." It was Ben's voice. "His name is Nick and they ordered the chocolate mousse…or was it crème brûlée?" he asked in a serious voice.

"You're just jealous. Because nobody wants to share crème brûlée with you," Luanne replied tartly.

Speak for yourself, Carey wanted to say.

Luanne tossed a pot holder at her brother and he fended it off with his arm, laughing at her.

He had come in the back door and they hadn't even noticed, Carey realized. He wore the same gray pullover and jeans as he'd had on that morning, with a dark red down vest on top.

Carey hoped he hadn't heard the earlier part of the conversation, when his sister had divulged his entire romantic history.

He walked up to the worktable and glanced down at their dishes. "Are you guys having lunch? Why didn't anyone call me?"

She met Ben's amused gaze and knew that he and his sister were just teasing each other, verbally sparring the way siblings do. They seemed a little old for it, but perhaps brothers and sisters never quite grew out of the habit.

"Guess I'll have to jump in the car and grab something through a window. Some of that stuff is pretty good… They have these wraps with fried chicken bits inside," he explained to Carey.

"Ben, if you wanted to make me sick to my stomach, you've succeeded. Just the thought of that stuff… It will kill you. I'm not kidding. You don't eat that junk when you're at work, do you?"

Carey knew Ben was just trying to push Luanne's buttons and had aptly succeeded.

Luanne stood up and stared him down. "What do you want? A sandwich? I'll fix it for you. How about roast beef with brie? I have some nice hot sourdough bread."

Ben rubbed his chin, looking thoughtfully at the ceiling. "Can I get fries with that?"

Carey laughed. "Ben, stop teasing her. You're going to miss out on a gourmet lunch."

He glanced at Carey and nodded. "Yeah, you're right. I definitely could not get anything like that through a little window."

While Luanne began to fix Ben's lunch, he sat down at the

chrome table across from Carey. "What are you doing hanging around the kitchen? Picking up some cooking tips?"

Even Luanne's tips probably couldn't help her, Carey thought. She was pretty hopeless in the kitchen. But she didn't need to tell Ben that.

"I'm helping Luanne polish up her new menu. Everything sounds great. I think you'll be mobbed with customers."

Luanne glanced at Ben. "That would be a miracle."

"My sister is a brilliant chef. But her sophisticated recipes aren't exactly winning over hearts and palates around here. Unfortunately for us."

Carey shrugged. "Everyone loves good food. Maybe you need a few reviews or advertisements to get people to notice the place."

"We were hoping for that, once we got the new menu ironed out." Luanne brought Ben's sandwich to the table and set it down in front of him. "We're going to contact some local newspapers and radio stations that do restaurant reviews and invite them in. We'll say it's a grand reopening or something. We might even change the name of the dining room. Give it a face-lift."

"That's a good idea," Carey agreed.

Ben didn't answer. He took a bite of his sandwich, his expression turning serious. Luanne had noticed it, too.

"Ben doesn't think we should advertise. He thinks it's tacky."

"I never said that," he argued back.

Luanne ignored him. "My dad never advertised. He always said, if you had a good product, people would find you. He thought advertising was a waste of money and somehow cheapened the place. But our mother has some different ideas about it."

Ben put his sandwich down, half-eaten. "This is all Walter's idea, Luanne. You know it and so do I. He's talked her into everything—the new menu, higher room rates, redecorating…"

"So? What's the problem? This place needs a push, Ben. If we don't do something, we're not going to stay in business."

"I don't disagree. I just don't want to see everything changed so much it feels like the chain hotel on the highway. And where is the money coming from? A loan, probably. A big one, I'd guess…"

"It's none of your business, Benjamin Ward Martin. I've told you that before."

Thea stood at the other side of the long chrome table, facing down her son. "When you're ready to work here full-time, 24/7, as I do, then these decisions will all be up to you. I'd be happy to step aside."

Ben didn't reply. He crossed his arms over his chest and leaned back in his chair. "Mother, this isn't the place or the time to have this discussion. Again."

"I have to start prepping for dinner service," Luanne announced. Two more kitchen helpers had just walked in and were hanging up their coats near the back door, Carey noticed. "So you folks need to take this somewhere else, okay?"

Carey glanced around quickly at everyone's sullen expressions. She felt very awkward, in the middle of something private, though it certainly wasn't her fault.

Lindsay made a fussing sound, waking up, and Carey quickly picked the baby up out of her bed.

Perfect timing, she silently noted.

Thea let out a long breath. She appeared to agree with her children, and didn't say anything more.

She walked over to Carey, who now held the baby up on her shoulder. "Did she have a good nap? I guess we woke her up with our haggling. I'm sorry…"

"She slept long enough. She'll go down again this afternoon," Carey said. "I can help you with the mailing later. I'm just going to change Lindsay's diaper."

Take a look at what's on offer at

www.millsandboon.co.uk

"Whenever you're able. But what about Lindsay? She's up now. I think she wants to play," Thea said as Lindsay reached out and tugged on one of Carey's earrings.

Carey glanced over her shoulder at Ben. "Maybe Ben can bring the portable crib down to the office. She can play in there while I'm at the computer."

"Good idea. I'll play with her awhile," Thea offered. "I just have a few phone calls to take care of this afternoon. Walter is going to drop by later."

Ben rose and put his plate in the sink. "I found another one of those folding cribs in the storage room. I'll set it up in the office for you."

"Thanks. I'll be down in a little while." Carey glanced at him as she left the kitchen, but he seemed to be avoiding eye contact with her. Or was that just her imagination?

Maybe he felt embarrassed about her witnessing the family argument?

She had the vague feeling he disapproved of her helping his mother and sister with hotel business. She thought he would be pleased to see her trying to repay them for their generosity. Not angry at her.

But she'd now caught a glimpse of certain tensions in the Martin family. Maybe he thought she was siding with his sister and mother against him, in some strange way? Which was silly.

She had no opinion one way or the other about how the inn should be run or renovated. She was just trying to be helpful and she was only going to be here a few more days. It shouldn't matter to Ben one way or the other.

Or to her, she reminded herself.

Carey spent the rest of the day in the hotel office, sending out the new brochures and even fielding phone calls whenever Thea stepped away, or was busy playing with Lindsay.

The afternoon went by quickly and she enjoyed learning more about how the inn was run. She began to see the place as a kind of theater, with a backstage area, where all the work went on behind the scenes. And a front stage, where the guests were served and pampered, and everything seemed to go smoothly, without strain or effort.

Thea was a genuinely warm and vivacious woman, Carey thought, but she was also playing the part of the hospitable, courteous innkeeper, eager to make all her guests feel welcome and special. She was quite a good actress, Carey realized as she watched Thea deal with different guests and their problems and questions. She had to be, to give the inn a distinctive personality.

She wondered what Ben's father, James, had been like. There was a photo of James in the office and Carey could see that Ben did greatly resemble him. Thea had said Ben's father was stubborn, but Carey guessed from the photo that he also had a lighter, humorous side. Again, a lot like his son.

Walter Flynn arrived in the late afternoon. Carey was at the computer, adding some additional names and addresses to the mailing list. Thea was sitting in an armchair near her desk, with Lindsay on her lap, playing a game of peekaboo with a big woolen hat.

Carey couldn't help but notice how Walter walked into the office as if he worked there, too. Thea greeted him with a warm smile and he bent to kiss her cheek. "Walter, I didn't expect you so early," she said, seeming surprised to see him.

He lifted his wrist and checked his watch. "I think I said I'd be here at five. It's already a quarter past," he noted. "You must have been very busy today. You lost track of time."

"I wasn't that busy. But we did have fun back here today. Carey's been helping me with the brochure. We're almost ready to send it out," Thea reported happily. "She made some very nice changes, too. Take a look."

She showed him a copy of the newest version and Walter looked quite impressed. "Nice job. This looks very polished now. That's what we're aiming for. Thank you so much."

"It wasn't much…you're welcome," she added. She wondered why Walter should be thanking her. He sounded as if he had an important place here.

Yet, from what she'd overheard in the kitchen, he had no special rights beyond his relationship with Thea—or rather, his influence over her, to hear Ben tell it. But that was considerable, Carey realized.

She'd only seen them together briefly at the Christmas dinner. But now she could tell that they were in a serious relationship. Which she thought was nice for Thea, who clearly missed her husband and had so much responsibility on her shoulders.

It was good for her to have companionship, Carey thought, someone she could talk to and trusted. Aside from Ben and his sister. Though it seemed Ben didn't approve of his mother's choice. Or maybe nobody would be good enough to replace his father.

Carey noticed again that Walter was quite well dressed, looking very dapper in a gray suit, light blue button-down shirt and a yellow tie. A few years older than Thea, she would guess, he was still an attractive man.

He did appear to be a completely different type of man than Thea's late husband, James. So this time, she'd been drawn by the opposite type. At least, from what Carey could judge from James Martin's picture and from what she'd heard… And from knowing Ben, who Thea insisted was a lot like his father.

Walter was also drawn by the baby and took her from Thea, into his lap. Lindsay had rarely enjoyed so much attention and seemed to be basking in it. She doesn't even seem to notice I'm in the room, Carey thought. She supposed that this was the way children behaved with their grandparents. But Lindsay had not been fortunate that way.

"I have those furniture catalogs we sent for, Thea," Walter said. "And the fabric mill finally sent a few material samples. I wasn't impressed with the quality. But you see what you think... Oh, my. She's got my tie now. She's a little tiger, isn't she?"

Walter grinned, looking to Thea to rescue him from Lindsay's assault.

"Wait...I have something for her. Let me go find it." Thea checked a supply closet in the rear of the room and pulled out a bottle of bubble liquid and a small plastic wand.

"Do you ever blow bubbles for her, Carey? Babies this age love it."

Carey looked up from the computer screen. She noticed that she was almost to the bottom of the list. Though it sounded as if Walter and Thea had better things to do than amuse Lindsay, it didn't make sense to leave until she was done.

"No...I don't think so. Maybe in the bathtub," Carey said.

"Watch this." Thea dipped the wand into the bottle and blew out a few small bubbles that floated in Lindsay's direction. Lindsay's eyes grew incredibly wide, following their flight. Then she reached out and batted at the crystal orbs with her hands. Walter held her tightly on his lap, while he laughed quietly.

When the bubbles had popped, she flapped her arms up and down, squealing with excitement. She stared at Thea, expectantly.

"She's very bright," Thea said. "More? Do you want some more, sweetie?"

Thea dipped the wand again and Lindsay watched the next flock of bubbles with a fascinated expression.

"She's trying to figure it all out. Just like the rest of us," Walter said philosophically.

"Good point, Walter." Ben strolled into the office and

glanced down at his mother and Walter, playing with the baby. "I'm nearly thirty-five and I don't have a clue."

Carey stopped typing and met his glance. His expression didn't reveal much, but something in his eyes seemed to light up when he saw her. She felt a secret thrill at the way he just looked at her.

"Are you done for the day, Ben?" Thea asked him. "We're going in for dinner soon. Luanne is serving a few of the new items on the menu tonight. She wants us to taste test. Carey…would you like to join us? We can all eat together," Thea suggested.

But before Carey could answer, Ben replied, "I was just about to leave for Highland. There are a few things I need at that big hardware warehouse near the mall."

"Oh." Thea seemed disappointed. She and Walter exchanged a look and Carey guessed they thought Ben was purposely avoiding Walter's company.

"Why don't you go later in the week? It's not an emergency, is it?"

"By next week there will be other things to fix," he said. No one could argue with that. He turned to Carey. "Would you like to come with me, Carey? I think you need to be rescued out of this office."

Thea looked suddenly cheerful again.

"Good idea. Poor Carey. She's been stuck here all afternoon. You two go to Highland and shop, and grab a bite to eat somewhere. Lindsay can stay with us. Walter and I will watch her," she offered. "Right, Walter?"

Thea did not actually kick Walter in the shin, but he seemed to jump up as if she had, Carey noticed.

"Absolutely. No trouble at all. Delightful child," he responded as if on cue.

"Well…that settles it. I guess I'm going to Highland." Carey's tone was dry, ironic. No one seemed to notice.

Ben seemed pleased, though his smile was guarded. They decided to meet in the lobby in fifteen minutes. Carey needed some time to get the baby settled with Thea, to give her all the necessary instructions and supplies.

And a few more minutes to fix herself up for this unexpected outing. What did a girl wear for a date to a hardware warehouse anyway? She had no idea….

Chapter Seven

It was already dark outside when Carey and Ben left the inn. They drove down Main Street, where streetlights glowed in the winter twilight and shops were closing for the day.

Carey watched out her window as the storefronts passed from view and Ben turned onto the road that led to the highway.

"You're quiet, Carey. Is something wrong?"

"Just unwinding. It feels a little strange leaving Lindsay. I'm so used to having her with me."

"She'll be fine, don't worry. My mother is great with babies."

"I can see that."

They hadn't driven very far at all or even gotten on the highway, when Ben pulled into a large parking lot. Carey saw a large, rustic-looking restaurant with a painted sign in front. The Steer Barn. The lot was crowded and she guessed the place served good food.

She suddenly realized she should have known they weren't

really going to a hardware warehouse. Or even going to Highland. Wherever that was.

They got out of the SUV and Ben led her toward the entrance, his arm circling her shoulder in a gesture that made her feel warm and happy inside.

"I love my sister's cooking. But sometimes a guy craves some plain old meat and potatoes. No goat cheese. No baby arugula. No…béarnaise sauce. Know what I mean?"

Carey laughed. "I do know what you mean."

And Ben did seem a "meat and potatoes" sort of guy, if she stopped to think about it.

"So that urgent need to visit the hardware store in Highland…just a cover story?"

"I didn't want to hurt anyone's feelings. And I had to think of some way to get you out of there. Away from my family."

So they could spend some time alone together, Carey silently finished for him. She felt the same. She glanced up at him and smiled, her senses stirred by his nearness.

They walked inside where a hostess greeted them, then led them to a table in a quiet corner. Ben helped her off with her jacket and held out her chair.

The room was dimly lit with a low beamed ceiling. The tables were set with crisp linen, sparkling crystal and white china. A candle on their table cast an intimate glow.

"This is a steak house, I gather?" Carey said, opening her menu.

"Best beef for fifty miles in any direction," he promised. "Are you hungry?"

She nodded. "Yes, I am."

"Great. We can share the porterhouse…and a bottle of Cabernet."

"Don't forget the potatoes," Carey reminded him.

"I wouldn't dare. And some French-fried onion rings, I think…"

She peeked at him over the menu and caught him smiling at her. "Just don't tell Luanne I brought you here. She'll never forgive me. In her book, this place is almost as bad as fast food."

"Don't worry. Your secret is safe with me," she promised. Just another secret to keep, she realized. She had quite a few of them.

A waitress arrived and they ordered. She soon returned with a bottle of wine and poured out two glasses.

"My mother has you busy the last two days, I noticed. She's not that good with office work. You've been a big help to her."

"I don't mind. I have nothing else to do and it makes the day go faster."

"You're a good sport to help her out. And Luanne. They have some big plans about changing the inn. I'm not so sure it's all going to work out." His tone was casual, but Carey sensed a much deeper concern.

"How long has your family run the inn? Did your father start it?"

"He took it over from his father." He paused and took a sip of his wine. "The business has been in the family four generations. My great-grandfather bought the mansion from a man who owned a textile mill, just after the Civil War."

"I can understand why it means so much to all of you." She paused, not knowing if she should ask him the question that came to mind. "Did you ever think of running it, Ben? Your mother sounds as if she wouldn't mind."

He looked surprised, then shook his head, smiling slightly. "So she claims. Especially in an argument. I'd like to see her let go that easily." He sighed and sat back in his chair. "Of course, I've thought about it. Especially after my father died. But I love what I do. I'm not ready to give up being a law officer. I love the inn…but I don't know if I'd really enjoy running it. Not on my own," he added.

He glanced at her a moment, then looked down at his glass. She had a feeling he didn't mean without his sister, Luanne. He meant without a wife.

"I was married for a few years," he said suddenly. "It didn't work out."

"I did hear that you were divorced. Someone at the Christmas party mentioned it," Carey said. "Why didn't it work?" she asked, curious to hear his version of the story.

Ben shrugged. "We met in college. Maybe we got married too young. She wanted something different from life than I did. Someone different," he added, his tone taking on a rough edge. "The worst part was being lied to. She just should have been honest with me. It could have been a lot easier for everyone."

Carey heard the bitter note in his voice and felt her breath catch in her throat. Honesty wasn't always easy. And sometimes, it seemed plain impossible, she wanted to say.

While she was glad Ben had finally told her about his past, it also pained her to hear him talk about his ex-wife's deception. Carey knew she was guilty of the same failing.

If she had any conscience or ethics at all, she'd get up and walk right out of the restaurant. And never have anything to do with him again.

But of course, she didn't do that. She just couldn't.

She looked up and met his brilliant blue eyes. She reached across the table and took his hand. She twined her fingers with his. "I'm sorry, Ben."

She knew that he thought she was talking about his failed marriage. But she meant so much more.

He looked surprised by the gesture and didn't say anything. Then he leaned over and softly kissed her, his lips lingering, savoring the touch.

"Carey, when you look at me that way, I can't remember that anything unhappy ever happened to me. I can hardly remember my name," he added with a small, sexy smile.

She knew just what he meant. She felt exactly the same every time she was near him.

He leaned closer, about to kiss her again, when the waitress appeared with their dinner.

Saved by the porterhouse, she silently quipped. For now, at least.

While they ate their meal, Carey asked him questions about his police work and the other men on the force. Ben had a lot of amusing tales of small-town police work. Though there were stories of real criminals and serious danger, too.

Carey felt too full for dessert or even coffee. Ben agreed. He paid the bill and they walked outside, huddling together in the chilly night air. He slipped his arm around her shoulder and held her close. She leaned against him and put her arm around his waist.

When they reached the car, he kissed her quickly, then opened her door. "Better get in. Or they'll find us frozen like ice sculptures in the morning."

She laughed, then slipped inside. He got in the driver's side and started the engine.

"We can still make the hardware store," he teased her. "It's open until midnight."

"That's all right. I'm getting a little old for those wild nightspots."

"I know what you mean." He laughed quietly, then reached over in the darkness and took her hand. "Okay, I have a better idea. We're not very far."

They drove along the road for a while and then Ben suddenly turned into an even narrower road, and then it seemed as if they were driving down a path in the woods.

Carey's eyes slowly adjusted to the darkness. The moon was nearly full and shining brilliantly in a clear, inky-blue sky.

All she could see were trees.

"Do you know where were are?" she asked quietly.

He laughed. "Don't be scared. I come here all the time. It's my favorite place. I want you to see it."

She sat quietly, waiting. Wondering what she was going to see.

Finally, the narrow road opened. The tree trunks thinned out. The vehicle stopped and Carey saw they were on the top of a mountain, looking down at a fabulous view—a wide, frozen lake, ringed by tall pines, shining in the moonlight.

Ben shut the engine and then the car lights. It was very dark and quiet. Then slowly her eyes adjusted and she saw the silvery, magical beauty. The sky above seemed to be filled with a million stars. More than she'd ever seen in her life.

"It is beautiful. It looks…enchanted here or something."

"Doesn't it?"

He put his arm around her shoulder and she moved close to him, leaning her head on his chest.

"I come here sometimes, just to think."

"What do you think about?" she asked quietly.

"The past. Mistakes I've made. Things I could have done differently. I think about the future, too. Things I hope for."

When he spoke, she felt his words, the echo in his broad chest. She heard his heartbeat steady and strong.

"What do you hope for, Ben?"

He didn't answer at first. She wondered if he was going to confide in her. Was she the one asking too many questions now?

"Oh…lots of things," he said finally. "I'd like to meet someone I can be happy with. Someone I can just be myself with." He turned to her. "Someone like you, Carey."

His arms circled her body and he pulled her closer. Their gazes met for a moment before his mouth met hers in a deep, smoldering kiss. There was nothing hesitant or coaxing about the way he kissed her. He jumped in, headfirst. Carey followed, as if diving into the inky darkness that surrounded them.

They kissed each other hungrily, struggling to get closer. It seemed apparent to each of them, simultaneously, that their heavy down jackets had to go. Carey shed hers in a second and pushed it aside, then helped Ben.

They were quickly in each other's arms again, feeling even closer and warmer. Kissing and touching with feverish urgency.

"Are you cold?" he whispered in her ear.

She felt his hands moving over her, slipping under her sweater, gliding over her bare skin.

"I'm fine. I'm…perfect…"

She sighed into his mouth, then quietly gasped as his hand glided over her breast, teasing the tip to an aching peak. A surge of heat swept through her body and she took a deep breath.

She was eager to touch him, too. She unbuttoned the top of his shirt and pressed her mouth to his warm skin. Then slipped her hands underneath, caressing his muscular back and rock-hard stomach.

He sighed and shuddered, his head leaning back a moment. Then he gently pushed her back on the seat and whisked her sweater over her head.

She was shocked by the cold air for a moment, until his body covered hers again. His head dipped down and his warm lips trailed a path of kisses over her soft silky skin. He pushed the straps of her bra aside and his mouth covered the taut peak of her breast, his tongue working wild magic, until she writhed in pure pleasure, melting inside with longing.

Her hand glided over his long lean thighs and she felt him hard and ready to make love. She heard him draw in a quick, harsh breath as she touched him. Then he covered her hand with his own, and brought her palm to his lips.

"As desperate as I am to be with you, I don't want it to happen in the backseat of a car." His fingers trailed through her hair. He cupped her cheek with his hand. "We could go back to my house... We're not far."

The question hung in the air between them. Carey felt her heart skip a beat. She knew what he was asking and what she would be agreeing to. Her mouth went dry.

She wanted him so much. Just to be close to him for a stolen hour or two.

It was hard to say no. It was hard to say anything.

Finally, she sat back and started putting on her clothes. She didn't look at him. "I want to...but I don't think it's a good idea. I'm leaving in a few days. If we get involved with each other, it will just make it harder."

He stared straight ahead and didn't say anything. She wondered if he was angry at her, then realized he was just surprised. And hurt, maybe.

"I thought we were already involved," he said finally. "I know we just met. But I can't help what I feel. I think you feel the same. Don't you?"

She sighed. She couldn't deny it. She had real feelings for him, deep feelings that had come so fast. The way people said it happened sometimes. As if she'd known him forever. As if they were meant for each other. Meant to be together...always.

But she couldn't let her thoughts run off in that direction.

"It's not that simple. Not for me. I can't just make love with you...and leave."

"Portland isn't so far. It doesn't have to be the end when you go," he said quietly.

"I don't think that would work out. Long-distance things never work for me. Portland is probably temporary. I don't even know where I'll end up. Eventually."

That was true enough.

He didn't answer right away. Then he turned and looked at her.

"Is there something you're not telling me, Carey?"

She felt her heart suddenly pound and wondered if he could hear it.

Did he have suspicions about her? Had he figured out that she wasn't who she claimed?

"What do you mean? Not telling you…about what?"

"Is there someone else? Another man?"

She shook her head. "No…there's no one. That's not why."

"What about Paul? The friend you were talking to on the phone this morning?"

She shook her head, feeling so relieved, she nearly laughed out loud. "He's just a friend. He and his wife, Nora. He used to work with Tom and they helped me after Lindsay was born. They're like parents in a way. I miss them," she added.

"I see. I guess I got the wrong impression. The way you sounded when you talked to him."

So he had overheard some of her conversation. But he'd thought it was a boyfriend. He wasn't thinking about anything else.

"It's all right." She reached out and rested her hand on his shoulder.

She loved touching him, loved the feeling of his warm, solid body under her hands. She could touch and explore him all night…if things were different.

But it wouldn't be right to give in to her desire. It wouldn't be fair to him. Every kiss, every touch, every caress between them would be just another lie. Another deception.

"I've betrayed your trust enough, Ben," she wanted to say. "Believe me, I'm doing you a favor."

Instead, she said, "I'm sorry. It's just not the right timing. My life is just…too confusing right now. I wish it was different, Ben. I really do."

He sighed and looked straight ahead. Then his expression looked suddenly resigned.

"I understand. You don't have to say anything more. We'd better get back. It's getting late."

He started the engine and pulled on his seat belt. Carey tugged her jacket back on and stared out her window.

She had just rejected the most wonderful, caring, sexy, compellingly attractive man she'd met in a very long time.

Very possibly, in her entire life.

She'd just pushed him away. As if it didn't matter to her at all.

A man she felt happy just to be with. Who understood her, without any effort at all. Someone who thrilled her with just a look. Or a smile.

Someone she could really love.

Had she already fallen in love with him? Maybe she had, she realized. It could happen that way.

But not for her.

Carey felt herself utterly alone again, staring into a huge, black void. She suddenly felt so empty and sad. She pressed her hands together in her lap and forced herself not to cry.

She didn't want Ben to see her this way. He could never understand how hard this was for her.

How much this hurt her, too.

The next two days passed with no word from Ben. Carey kept expecting him to drop by the inn to fix something, or just to visit his family. But he never came. She listened for his name in conversations, but his sister and mother barely mentioned him.

Walking through the village each day with Lindsay, she looked for his police car. She knew she shouldn't but couldn't help it. She even thought she spotted his cruiser on Main Street once, but it turned down a side street before she could tell for sure.

She busied herself helping Thea. Ben's mother always seemed over her head with some new project she'd taken on, or wanted Carey's opinion on some pressing question.

Carey helped Thea sort out her monthly accounts, which were, not surprisingly, a tangled mess. Carey knew a great deal about bookkeeping and showed Thea how to put her records on the computer. Thea already had the software and didn't even realize it.

"I'm sure I seem like a complete airhead," Thea apologized. "This was all my late husband's territory. Paying the bills, doing the payroll, making schedules for employees. I've been struggling along with it all since we cut back on the office help. But not doing a very good job, I'm afraid."

"Maybe you ought to hire someone to help. Even a few hours a week," Carey suggested.

Thea sighed. "I've thought of that. Maybe after the renovation." Thea slowly smiled at her. "Of course, if you ever had second thoughts about working for your friend, I'd hire you in a heartbeat, Carey. Would you ever consider staying and working here?"

Carey was surprised by Thea's offer. She didn't know what to say. What a nice ending to her story that would be. Working at the inn, living in Greenbriar…having a relationship with Ben…

But, of course, that was impossible. She was living on borrowed time here, expecting to be discovered and unmasked at any minute. If she stayed here with the Martins, sooner or later, they would all find out how she had lied about her identity and how she was even wanted now in connection with a crime.

Carey saw her pleasant fantasy burst, like the floating bubbles Thea made for Lindsay.

"That's very flattering, Thea…but I've promised my friend I'd come and help her. She's counting on me."

"Of course. I understand. Just remember, if it doesn't work out, you can always come back here."

The offer made Carey feel wanted and special. But also saddened her. She wondered if Thea's plans were going to succeed. Ben wasn't so optimistic. But he also kept himself at a safe distance, she noticed.

When the hard work of straightening out the accounts was over, Thea was ready for a more creative project. She pulled out a pile of furniture catalogs, fabric samples and wallpaper books, some of which Walter had brought over the other night.

"Can you take a look at these with me, Carey, and tell me what you think?"

She spread the books out on a big table. The pages were covered with yellow stickies, Carey noticed. They had already been studied carefully. "Walter tries, but he isn't much help. Everything he shows me is either brown or dark green. Most men like those colors. I think it has something to do with being color-blind…don't you?"

Thea showed Carey pictures of room settings and wall colors, discussing her ideas for renovating.

"We don't want to get too contemporary and lose the historic feeling. But we need to clear out the stuffiness. Some of these rooms have looked the same since the Civil War, for goodness' sake."

Carey gave her opinions and helped Thea figure out the costs of suppliers and different materials and furnishings, which was a difficult but important part of the process.

"They have decorators who specialize in hotels and do this sort of thing for you. For a fee, of course. Which we can't afford right now," Thea added.

"I don't think you need to worry, Thea. Your ideas are great and you have terrific taste," Carey said.

Thea looked pleased by the compliment. "I'm not very good at balancing a checkbook. But I do know how to pull a room together. Among other things," she added.

On Sunday afternoon, the inn was practically empty, with all the weekend visitors checking out soon after breakfast. Thea went out with Walter to visit his daughter, down in Kennebunkport.

Carey offered to watch the front desk, at least until five o'clock. The extra portable crib was still in the office and it wasn't any trouble to have Lindsay with her there.

It wasn't much different than sitting up in her room with Lindsay. She mostly read a book. But the activity in the lobby and the occasional phone call provided some distraction from thoughts of Ben.

Her car would be finished tomorrow. Harry Anderson reported it was right on schedule. She could probably leave some time in the afternoon. She wondered if she'd see Ben. Or even speak to him before she had to go. She wondered if she should call him. But if he really didn't want to speak to her, or have any more contact after their date at the steak house had ended so miserably… She knew she'd hate to hear a bitter note in his voice, or have him act coldly toward her.

She was just about to go up to her room and start her packing, when a call came in. She picked it up and answered. "Greenbriar Inn. Can I help you?"

"Carey…is that you?"

It was Ben. Carey felt a rush, her heart started racing.

"Yes, it's me," she said slowly. "Is this…Ben?"

"Of course it is. What are you talking about?"

"We haven't spoken in a while. I wasn't sure."

Her tone was innocent and perfectly serious.

"I thought you must have left town by now. Isn't your car ready yet?"

"It will be done tomorrow. Didn't Harry Anderson tell you?"

"I haven't asked Harry about your car," he insisted.

"Sure. Of course not," she said dryly.

"Is my mother there? I need to speak to her, please."

"She's out for the evening. Would you like to leave a message?" Carey's tone was efficient and polite. Infuriatingly so, she hoped.

"No. Thank you. I'll call back tomorrow."

"Shall I leave that message for her then?"

"All right. If it makes you happy, go ahead."

She was getting to him. She could tell. He deserved it.

He had some nerve kissing her the way he had, practically making love to her in the front seat of his truck…asking her to come back to his house….

Then not a word. Three whole days.

He had some nerve.

"Anything else?" she challenged him.

There was a long silence. She wondered if he was still there.

"You have a safe trip, Carey. Don't drive into any wildlife."

"I'll try to remember that. Thanks for the tip," she said tartly. Tears welled up in her eyes. She forced herself not to cry.

"Well…goodbye." His voice was suddenly quiet, muffled sounding.

"Goodbye, Ben," she replied quickly. Then she hung up.

So that was that.

It could have been so much more. But Carey didn't allow herself to imagine what might have been.

Chapter Eight

Thea decided to close the inn on New Year's Eve and New Year's Day. In years past, she explained to Carey, they not only stayed opened but served a special dinner with music and dancing, champagne, confetti and noisemakers at midnight. There wasn't enough interest this year, though, to warrant it.

In the old days, the inn would be filled to capacity with so many of the couples at the party staying over. On New Year's Day, they would serve their famous "Hair of the Dog" brunch.

"Which actually was a lot more appetizing than it sounds, dear," Thea clarified. "People could not get enough of my husband's special, 'hangover-Rx' Bloody Marys."

Carey buttered a piece of bread, then handed it to Lindsay, who sat in a high chair next to the table. She and the baby had joined Thea and Luanne for breakfast and they were eating at the long chrome worktable in the kitchen.

"Sounds like quite a bash."

"Oh…it was." Thea's tone was wistful. "It was a *real* fun, no-holds-barred party. Not just a pleasant little get-together."

Carey guessed that Thea was referring to the New Year's Eve party she would be attending with Walter, hosted by his former business partner at the insurance agency, who was now retired and lived quite a distance away. They planned to stay overnight. Not that it would be a late night, or include much revelry, Thea noted.

"The party tonight won't be much," Thea confessed. "We pair off for bridge, then have a toast at midnight. I'm not a very good player. I usually give away my hand. But Walter puts up with me." She sighed.

Luanne also had plans. She was going to visit her boyfriend, Nick, in Portland and spend the holiday with him, even though he had to work. His boss didn't mind an extra cook in the kitchen, not on such a busy night.

Luanne's overnight bag was already set near the back door and she was dressed for traveling in slim-fitting black pants and a sapphire-blue velvet blazer. Her long hair was brushed out loose and shiny, and a light touch of makeup brought out her beautiful blue eyes and flawless complexion.

Carey had rarely seen the chef out of her kitchen whites. The change was remarkable. Like on a TV makeover show, she thought. Of course, Luanne didn't see her boyfriend much and wanted to look her best.

Carey didn't have anyone to dress up for tonight. Or…anytime in the near future, for that matter. She tried hard not to think about Ben but couldn't help it. He probably knew both his sister and mother would be leaving early today for their holiday and now he had no excuse at all to drop by.

After their tart telephone conversation, she didn't really expect to see him before she left anyway.

"I'm going to miss you, Carey." Luanne pulled her close for

a farewell hug. "Maybe you can come visit in the summer? Your friend will give you some vacation time, I hope."

Carey nodded. She couldn't stand lying to these lovely, sweet people anymore. "Have a good time in Portland," she said, avoiding Luanne's question entirely. "I really enjoyed getting to know you. I hope you have a great New Year."

"You, too. Keep in touch, okay?"

Again, Carey didn't answer. But Luanne didn't wait to hear one. She was in a great hurry now to leave, so she could be with Nick. She grabbed her bags and exchanged a quick farewell with Thea.

After Luanne was gone, the cavernous kitchen seemed very quiet. Thea glanced at her watch. "I'd better get moving, too. What time will your car be ready? Did he say?"

"Sometime this afternoon."

"Oh…I was hoping it would be done earlier. Walter wants to leave by noon. He's concerned about traffic. I won't be around to help you pick the car up."

"That's okay. I can walk down to the village with Lindsay and get it by myself. Then I'll drive back here and put my bags in."

Carrying the car seat to the gas station was going to be a pain in the neck, Carey realized. But she didn't want to trouble Thea anymore.

"You've helped me enough, Thea. Honestly," Carey added, and she meant it sincerely.

"It was nothing." Thea touched her arm. "I loved having you here. I'll miss you, Carey."

They cleared up the breakfast dishes together and Thea went back to her apartment. Carey brought Lindsay back up to their room and packed up a few belongings that were still scattered around.

Her cell phone rang. She thought it might be Harry, telling her the car was ready earlier than expected.

It was Paul. She was glad to hear his voice. She'd planned to call him later, when she was leaving town.

"Hello, Paul. I'm glad you called. My car will finally be done today and I'm all packed up to go."

"Good thing I caught you then. You'd better just stay put, Carey. Quinn's P.I.s have left New York. I don't know where they're looking for you now. I think you've found a good place to hide out. At least until I know what's what."

"I see…" Carey sat down on the bed. She felt confused and agitated. The tables were always being turned on her. She'd make a plan and could never follow through.

"The district attorney's office is looking for you, too."

Carey felt a knot of dread in the pit of her stomach at the news. Though she wasn't surprised.

"I found an old newspaper article about the case, at the library. It seemed just a matter of time before they got around to me."

"Listen, Nora and I were talking. Maybe you should come back. Turn yourself in to the district attorney. He might give you better treatment if you come forward willingly. If you're running from them, Carey, they assume you're guilty. But once they hear your story, they'll know you didn't have anything to do with Quinn's dirty work. I'll certainly speak up for you," he added.

Carey was sure he would. But not so sure that would help her any.

"I'm sure Quinn will tell them just the opposite, Paul. He'll make them believe the whole thing was my idea. Just to get back at me for leaving and then testifying against him. You know the way he is."

"I do, Carey, but please…just consider it. I don't think you can use that fake identification now at the border. I don't think it will hold up with the customs agents."

"I'm afraid, Paul. Not just for myself, but for Lindsay. If the district attorney doesn't believe me, I might go to jail if I come forward. What will happen to Lindsay? If Quinn isn't convicted, or gets off with a slap on the wrist, who will protect us? I'll still need to hide somewhere from him. At least this way, I'm getting a head start."

"I can't argue with you. I understand what you're saying. It's a hard choice to make. An impossible situation... But we're worried about you, Carey. We're not sure how long you can stay out there. If you can't get up to Canada, where is this going to end?"

Carey didn't answer. She didn't know. She only hoped that in time, she could go on to Canada. Or maybe south, to Mexico.

Or maybe board a plane and disappear somewhere far over the ocean.

"For now, just promise me you'll stay where you are," Paul said. "I think it's your best bet. Will you promise?"

Carey sighed. "Okay. If you say so. I think I can work it out. For a little while longer, anyway."

"Good." Paul sounded calm again. "I'll keep in touch...and Happy New Year. I hope things turn around for you, Carey. I really do."

They both knew she needed a miracle. But she welcomed his good wishes. Carey sent good wishes to Nora, then said goodbye and closed her phone.

She sat quietly on the bed, figuring out what she needed to do. Thea had already offered her a job and told her she was welcome to stay here. But if she did, that would mean seeing more of Ben, sooner or later.

Perhaps it was over for him, she thought. She hadn't seen him or heard from him the past few days. Perhaps it wouldn't be hard for him at all if she stayed.

It would still be hard for her, Carey thought.

She couldn't worry about Ben. This was her life. Her safety

and, more importantly, Lindsay's safety she was dealing with. If it was wiser to stay in Greenbriar, as Paul advised, then that's what she had to do.

She took Lindsay from her crib and went down to look for Thea. It wasn't quite noon and she doubted Thea would have left without saying goodbye.

She saw a suitcase near the front desk and found Thea watering the plants in the sunroom.

Thea smiled when she noticed Carey coming. But at the same time, she looked a little downcast.

"I'm glad you came down. I'm just about ready to go. I wanted to show you how to lock up when you leave later."

"Thea…I just had a call. There's been a change in my plans," Carey began carefully.

Oh, she hated so much to lie to Thea. It had always been hard to do this, but now…she had to really force herself to spin out these stories. To draw on every acting trick she'd ever learned in acting classes.

"Is it your car? Has there been some delay in the repairs?"

She tried to seem calm and natural. But she could barely look Thea in the eye. She hoped the older woman wouldn't sense that something was off with her story.

"Uh…no. It wasn't about the car. It was my friend. In Portland. Now she says the job has been filled. She couldn't wait for me. She doesn't think I should come there after all."

Thea's expression was sympathetic. "Oh, that's too bad. And you were counting on it. What a disappointment for you." Carey could see a light start to glow behind her blue eyes. "But then that means you're free to stay here now…I mean, if you want to."

"I do want to," Carey said sincerely. "Do you still want me to work for you?"

Thea nodded so quickly her long earrings jangled. "Absolutely. I'd be so relieved to have you here. You're so clear-headed, Carey. So capable...and organized."

When you lie and dissemble as much as I do, being organized is a real necessity, Carey wanted to explain.

"I'd be happy to try it out," she said carefully. "Though I can't say for sure how long I can stay."

"That's all right, dear. I understand. Your life is a bit in flux now. Just see how you like it. Why don't we work out the salary and other arrangements when I get back? Would that be all right with you?"

Carey quickly agreed. She was sure Thea would be too generous and knew she couldn't have asked for a more flexible, appreciative employer.

"Luanne will be happy to hear you're staying," Thea said. "And Ben, too," she added.

I wouldn't count on that, Carey wanted to reply.

They heard the front door open, signaling someone's arrival. Carey's heart skipped a beat, thinking it might be Ben.

Then Walter called out from the lobby. "Hello? Anyone around?"

"In here, Walter," Thea replied. He soon appeared in the doorway.

"Ready to go, dear?"

"In a minute. I have some good news. Carey is staying. She's going to work here, help me in the office." Thea rested her hand lightly on Carey's shoulder in an affectionate gesture.

Walter looked pleased by the announcement and Carey was relieved. She knew how much Thea deferred to his opinion.

"Well, that's a surprise. I can see you've been a big help to Thea the past week. Good news for the New Year," he added.

"Yes, very good news. I'm very pleased with the way this has worked out," Thea said, pouring the last bit of water into a large Boston fern. "It's positively...fortuitous."

It had been lucky for her, too, Carey realized. In more ways than she could ever explain to them.

A few minutes later, Carey stood in the lobby, holding Lindsay in her arms as she bid Thea and Walter a safe trip.

"I'm sorry now to leave you here all alone, Carey. Maybe I should call Luanne and ask her to come back?"

"Please don't call Luanne. She's been dying to see her boyfriend. Lindsay and I will be fine. You don't have to worry, Thea," Carey insisted.

"All right." Thea still looked concerned. "We'll be back early tomorrow. Call us if anything comes up. And you can always call Ben. Though I'm pretty sure he's working a double shift. I don't think he gets off until at least eleven."

Ben? He was the last person she'd call in an emergency.

After a few more last-minute instructions on staying at the inn by herself, Thea and Walter finally left. Carey closed the heavy front door behind them and, as per Thea's instructions, turned the lock.

Carey was not wary at all of staying alone in the empty inn. At least, not at first. She busied herself during the day picking up her car and caring for Lindsay. While the baby napped in the afternoon, she worked in the office, cleaning out a box of old files and inputting records into the computer program she'd set up for Thea.

Carey had no idea how long she'd end up staying in Greenbriar, but there was enough work here for a long time. She did feel as if Thea needed her help and wasn't just doing her another favor. Of course, she was grateful for the chance to earn some money. Her savings had been practically used up by the cost of the car repairs. While working here, she would also save on rent.

There were many benefits to the unexpected job. And drawbacks, too...

Night fell. Carey had little to occupy her and became more

conscious of being alone. Especially on New Year's Eve. She couldn't quite remember spending the holiday by herself and decided the best thing to do was just ignore it and treat it like any other night of the year.

She gave Lindsay a long bath, playing extra games with her in the tub. The baby was practically too drowsy to eat and fell asleep soon after her dinner. Carey fixed herself a sandwich then settled on her bed and turned on the TV. She flicked around the channels, as all the images of happy couples, kissing and waving happily at the cameras, was just too depressing.

Lindsay had been asleep for hours, her crib pushed into the smaller room of Carey's suite, so she wouldn't be disturbed by the television. Carey shut off the TV and picked up a book, a thick historical novel. It helped to lose herself in a good story at night, giving her less time to think about the dramas of her own life. When she finally looked up from the pages, feeling weary enough to sleep, the clock on the bedside table showed that it was nearly eleven-thirty.

She changed into her nightgown and robe and decided to make herself a cup of tea. Some way to bring in the New Year. Maybe she wouldn't even stay up for it. She didn't have anything to celebrate. If she had made it all the way to Canada, as she had planned, she would feel differently. But right now her future looked very bleak.

Of course, if she'd never gotten stuck here, she would never have met Ben. Despite the sour ending to their brief connection, Carey knew he had touched her someplace deep inside. She wouldn't easily forget him after she left. It would be hard to keep her distance from him while she stayed here.

She checked Lindsay in her bed. She was sound asleep. Carey headed downstairs to the kitchen. Despite Thea's instructions, she had not remembered to leave any lights on.

The hallways and lobby were dim and shadowy, bringing to mind images of fright movies about haunted hotels...and ghoulish guests....

She thought of the nightmare she often had, the one with the figure who chased her...who caught her...

You're being totally idiotic, Carey told herself.

Still, the grand old place did look a bit spooky in the dark. At the foot of the stairway, she switched on a small Tiffany lamp, then noticed she'd left a light on in the office by mistake. Well, that could stay until morning, she decided. Thea had told her to leave a few lights on downstairs. It seemed a good idea.

The sunroom was also dark, but shafts of bright moonlight streamed through the large windows, illuminating her way. Carey headed for the door that led to the kitchen.

She'd only walked a few steps when she heard the rustle of a potted plant nearby. A tall, broad-shouldered figure stepped out, blocking her way.

"Hold it. Right there," a deep voice commanded.

Carey jumped back. She may have even screamed, but she wasn't sure.

A flashlight beam swept over her. She shielded her eyes with her hand.

"Ben?"

She heard a long, exasperated sigh. Then saw him holster his gun. "Damn...it's you. I thought someone had broken in."

"What made you think that? Were you about to shoot me?"

He turned off the flashlight and switched on a lamp. The room was cast in a soft glow.

He glanced at her, his bold gaze sweeping down her body, taking in her long loose curls and the ample curves outlined by her thin silky nightgown and robe.

"Not if you gave in without a struggle."

She tugged at the belt of her robe, noticing the V-shaped

opening in front was gaping open. Ben looked as if he had noticed, too.

Carey tightened the belt on her robe. "How did you get in?"

"I have a key to the back door. I saw the light on in the office. That's the first place a burglar would go. My mother never leaves that light on. But there's always one on in the lobby and outside, at the front door. And both of those were out. The place just didn't look right."

"She gave me instructions about the lights. I forgot," Carey admitted.

"I thought you left for Portland. Harry said your car was done."

So, he had been checking up on her. That made her feel a little better.

"My friend called. The job she was holding had to be filled. She hired someone else and didn't think it was a good idea for me to come."

"Oh…too bad." His words were laced with sympathy, though his expression didn't match at all. He looked genuinely happy, she noticed. He leaned back, his arms folded over his broad chest. "So, what now?"

She licked her lips, a lump forming in the back of her throat. It shouldn't be so hard to tell him this part…it just was.

"Thea offered me a job here, at the inn. I'm going to stay. At least for a while," she added. "We'll see how it goes."

Her words trailed off. The way he was looking at her now made her mouth grow dry. His dark blue gaze locked with her own and she felt mesmerized, unable to move. Unable to breathe.

He slowly walked toward her and suddenly, he stood inches away. She tipped her head back to look up at him.

The china clock on the mantel chimed, piercing the silence with a thin, bright note. Carey glanced at the face. The two hands on the clock face had met at twelve.

Her voice was a husky whisper. "Happy New Year, Ben."

"Happy…"

He never finished his sentence.

He stared down at her and sighed, his brilliant blue eyes growing smoky with desire. She saw a thrilling light there. Thrilling and terrifying.

His big hands had already settled on her hips, pulling her into the heat of his body. His mouth crashed down on hers with passionate intensity, like two worlds colliding in space. The explosion and heat rocked Carey to her core.

She felt as if every nerve ending in her body had been touched by a live electric wire. He slipped his hands up, around her slim waist, then tugged free the belt on her robe. It slid to the floor, tangling at their feet. His mouth plundered hers with moist, hot kisses as his hands slipped under the edges of the robe, then up and down her body, outlining her soft, feminine curves. The thin nightgown was little barrier to the heat of his palms on her skin.

This is how you're keeping your distance? Good job, Carey, a small voice chided.

Carey sighed deep inside. She told herself to step back. To pull away while she had a chance.

"Carey…I want you so much…" His harsh, whispered words felt like the brush of rough velvet on her senses.

She couldn't answer. She could barely breathe.

Weak with longing, she dipped her head a moment, pressing her forehead to his hard chest.

Her soft sigh seemed to push him over the edge. His head dropped and their lips met again. Their kiss was explosive. Like lightning lighting up the night sky.

As Ben's mouth moved hungrily over hers, Carey went limp in his arms, surrendering to the pressure of his warm, firm lips on hers, his hard, hot body pressing against every inch of her own. He coaxed her to follow and she eagerly responded. Her mouth opened against his like a flower, their tongues twining in an intimate dance.

Carey hardly knew herself, her hands wandering from his broad shoulders to his muscular back, her entire body rising into his embrace, yearning to feel more of him, every hard masculine inch of his body, merging with her own.

This was it, a distant voice informed her.

The age-old dance, the most basic, primitive magic in the universe. The source of creation, the deepest, unknowable mystery. An attraction so powerful it short-circuits your mind; all logic, all reason, fades into space. Irrelevant. Laughable.

Ben's hands smoothed away the edges of her robe until it slid down her arms. His head dropped to her shoulder and he murmured her name against her bare skin. One hand cupped her breast, his hands lightly brushing her nipple to alert attention, and a tingling sensation telegraphed to every trembling limb.

She met his glance a moment, then took him by the hand, a few short steps to a long divan.

Their bodies were parted for barely a moment. Ben pushed down the straps of her nightgown and pressed his hot mouth to her breast. First one, then the other. Her nipples had hardened to aching points and the touch of his wet lips felt electric. A hot molten wave of pleasure swept through her, from head to toe. She clutched his shoulders, aching to feel more of his caresses.

"God, you're beautiful. You really are," he whispered hoarsely.

Ben sat down on the couch and drew her down next to him. He kissed her deeply, again and again. At some point, her nightgown had slipped down her body completely, ending up in a silky puddle on the floor.

She felt the cool air on bare skin as he showered her body with kisses, his long sensuous caresses doing magical things to her, smoothing up her thighs, between her legs, down her back.

She worked on the buttons of his shirt and quickly bared his chest. Her lips pressed to his hot skin, ridges of muscle covered with dark thick hair. Her mouth covered a flat male nipple and she felt him shudder in her arms, clutching her. She kept her lips there, working sweet torture as her hands moved lower, unbuckling his belt and opening up his pants.

She knelt by his side a moment, tugging off his pants and then his shorts, her hands sliding up and down his long hard legs. She stroked and teased him, her hands roaming hungrily over his beautiful male form, his long hard muscular legs, flat stomach and rigid manhood.

She wanted so much to give him pleasure, as much as he'd been giving her. She covered him with her hot mouth, driving him to the edge and felt his hands in her hair, trembling as he sweetly moaned. Carey knew a certain, rare female power as he melted for a moment, surrendering to her completely.

Then she felt him pull her up until she was lying across the couch next to him. His hands stroked and caressed her, his fingers outlining the graceful curve of her thigh, then dipping into the warm, honeyed center of her womanhood.

He sighed against her mouth, then kissed her deeply, all the while gliding his fingers inside and outside of her. Wave upon wave of hot pleasure broke over her body.

Breathless and aroused to a fevered pitch, Carey felt about to explode. Her hands firmly grasping Ben's slim hips, she urged him to move over her. She lifted her head and pressed her lips to his chest. She fitted herself even closer, desperate to feel him sink into her velvety heat. She ached to feel him inside her, so badly she couldn't speak.

She felt the wonderful weight of his body, pressing her down into the cushions. Then a quick movement, as he slipped on protection. He moved over her, settling between her soft thighs, covering her face with kisses. Their gazes met for a magical moment as he joined his body with hers.

He thrust himself inside of her and she rocked against him. He moved slowly. She could feel him holding back his power. Then the rhythm grew stronger as he moved deep inside.

It felt so perfect. So…indescribable.

Not in all her relationships had she ever responded quite like this. It was as if she'd broken through to a new level of sexual excitement and release. A new world.

Their bodies seemed perfectly in tune, moving in a synchronized dance of pure pleasure, wordlessly. Effortlessly. It was like making love in a dream. But this was no dream. It was hot and real and overwhelming.

The heat seemed to mount inside of her, until Carey felt she would explode. Wave upon wave of electrifying pleasure broke over her body as she reached pleasure's peak.

She trembled and shuddered, calling out Ben's name.

Her head dropped limply back against the pillow and she gasped for air.

Ben's mouth dipped down to her breast, his tongue twirling around her ultrasensitive nipple. "There's more," he whispered. "Don't give up on me yet, Carey…"

He moved inside of her, teasing and tempting.

Carey closed her eyes and wrapped her slim legs even tighter around his waist. She gave as good as she got, matching each thrust of his powerful body.

Higher and higher.

Rising to another astounding peak.

Until she could barely breathe…

She gripped his shoulders and moaned. Then felt herself shatter again, into tiny, sparkling fragments. Like the glowing embers floating down from the sky after an explosion of fireworks.

Almost at the very same second she heard Ben gasp and felt him topple over the edge of ecstasy. One powerful thrust, then he trembled for a long moment, finally collapsing into her arms.

They lay together silently. She listened to his deep breathing and felt his heart pounding, so close to hers.

Ben's damp cheek brushed her shoulder. She could feel the day's growth of dark beard on her skin, a sandpaper feeling that she cherished.

She stroked his thick hair and let her hand wander down his bare back. Finally, he lifted his head and stared down at her.

He brushed a curly strand off her cheek and slowly smiled. His wolfish grin flashed in the darkness.

"Good party. But you forgot the champagne."

She twisted her head around, resting her cheek on a silky fringed pillow. "I thought you were bringing it."

His blue eyes sparkled in the dark, deep dimples creasing his cheeks. "I can find some, if you like."

She didn't know when she'd ever seen a man who looked so ruggedly handsome, so totally delicious.

She slipped out from under him and scooped up her nightgown.

"Find two glasses while you're at it, and meet me upstairs in the bedroom."

He sat up, his hungry gaze fixed on her body as she shimmied into the nightgown and robe again.

"It's a waste of time to put those things back on. You know that, don't you?"

She strolled out of the room, glancing at him over her shoulder for a moment.

"But I enjoy it so much when you take them off, Ben. That's definitely part of the fun."

"Sweetheart," he called after her quietly, "the fun has barely begun."

Chapter Nine

Carey's eyes slowly opened. Her mouth felt dry as cotton. Her eyes felt scratchy. The first thing she saw was an empty champagne bottle, floating upside down in a silver bucket. Tilted crazily to one side.

Just the way she felt.

It all came back to her in a rush.

Making love with Ben in the sunroom. And again up here. Drinking champagne, talking, laughing. And making love again…

She turned her head on the pillow. He slept soundly beside her, his head cuddled into the pillow, the sheet riding low on his bare hips. A faint smile on his face.

His hair was mussed, he was badly in need of a shave and looked about as ragged as she felt. She'd never seen a more stunning piece of manhood in her entire life. A cup of coffee, a hot shower…she could jump back into bed and start all over. No problem.

Was that fair?

Carey sighed. Fair had nothing to do with it. Hadn't she learned that by now?

She slipped out of the bed, careful not to disturb him. She wrapped the robe around her bare body and tied the belt tightly. She didn't hear a sound from Lindsay's crib in the small, adjoining room. She peeked inside to find the baby sound asleep. Carey felt thankful for a few minutes to get her head together.

Down in the kitchen, she got some coffee going, making the brew extra strong.

She recalled Thea's description of her husband's hangover cure and wished there were some of that elixir handy. She sure could use a dose to clear her head. But the ache behind her eyes was minor, compared to the aches all over her body. She was definitely out of shape in the lovemaking department and had called upon muscles last night that had not seen action for years.

If ever, Carey realized with a blush.

Ben was a passionate, tender and challenging partner. The match had definitely sharpened her game. He was just plain unbelievable in bed. In the back of her mind, she'd known he would be. But the actual experience of it, her wildest fantasies coming true, had been…a revelation.

She should have known, from the moment she set eyes on him, this was going to happen. It felt so inevitable, so unavoidable. She'd always believed she had control over her choices in life, for better or worse. But making love to Ben…that had seemed beyond her control. Like trying to stop a runaway train.

What now?

The inevitable night of bliss led to the inevitable morning after. Just before drifting off to sleep in his arms, she had tried to understand what it all meant. At least, for the brief time she'd be staying here.

Could she dare to be this close to him, without giving away

her secrets? Without tripping on a lie, arousing his suspicions by dropping some clue that she wasn't at all who she claimed to be?

He was a law enforcement officer, for goodness' sake. And he wasn't stupid.

One night was…one splendid night. But to continue…she'd be playing with matches while perched on a pile of dynamite.

She'd been so deep in her worries, she hadn't even heard him come in. He walked up behind her and slipped his arms around her waist. She felt his warm mouth nuzzle her nape and then his warm strong body pressed down the length of her.

"Good morning. How long have you been up and around?"

She felt the urge to turn in the circle of his embrace and continue the conversation face-to-face. Lips touching lips… But she forced herself to resist and instead, slipped out of his embrace.

"Long enough to make some coffee. Want some?" She poured out a mug and handed it to him. Then took one herself.

She finally turned and looked at him. He was bare chested, worn jeans resting on his hips. He smiled at her and she felt her resolve melt.

"I just checked on Lindsay. She's still asleep."

"Thanks. I'm making her a bottle. I'd better go up and wake her in a minute. It's getting late."

"I didn't know you wanted her up. I would have brought her down." He sat down on a stool and sipped his coffee.

"That's all right. I can get her."

After we have a little talk, she added silently.

Carey felt her stomach curl with dread. This was not going to be easy.

She'd found a bottle of headache tablets and shook out two in her hand. Then tossed them back with a swallow of coffee.

"Headache?" Ben's expression was sympathetic.

"Head…and assorted body parts," she admitted with a reluctant grin.

He leaned back in his chair, looking very satisfied. She could tell what he was thinking…and it brought a wave of heat to her cheeks.

"I can't believe how late we slept."

"With good reason," he said, his eyes sparkling.

"Your mother and Walter will be back soon. I'd rather she didn't find us here…like this."

"Like what?" he asked innocently.

Like you spent the night scorching the sheets in my bed, she wanted to say.

"Like…you stayed over. With me," she added.

"You're embarrassed?" When she didn't answer, he said, "My mother is a very modern woman, Carey. I even think she'll be pleased. I think she's been trying to get us together."

Carey thought the same, but didn't say.

"I feel…awkward. That's all. The first night I'm left alone here, she comes back and I'm entertaining an overnight male guest. Her son, in fact." She paused and stared at him. "Awkward?"

He looked thoughtful, considering her perspective. "All right. I see what you mean. Though, believe me, there's no reason to be embarrassed. What if I get dressed, go out and get some stuff at the bakery…and come back, as if I was just dropping by to say hello?"

Carey sighed. She twirled a strand of hair between her fingers, a habit she had when she was nervous.

"The thing is, Ben, I think we need to talk. You know?"

She could see that a note of worry in her voice had set off his silent alarm system. He sat up, a serious expression falling over his features as if a curtain had dropped.

"Okay…there was little of that going on last night, as I recall," he said bluntly.

"The thing is," she started slowly, carefully choosing her words, "we have this amazing attraction to each other. And that's…good."

He nodded, crossing his arms over his chest. "Very good. I'd go as far as to call it…outstanding," he cut in.

"Yes, this outstanding attraction," Carey continued. "And I think we've both known for a while that something was going to happen, sooner or later. I mean, it felt…"

"Inevitable."

"Exactly." She nodded, feeling encouraged that he seemed to be following her train of thought. "So we acted on it. That was only natural."

"Natural? It was supernatural. I haven't had sex that good since…"

Carey turned her head and looked at him. "Too much information."

He sat back. "Go on… You were saying?"

She leaned forward, but didn't dare to look at him. This was so hard. How could she do it?

Why was she doing it?

If it was just me, running from Quinn and the law, I'd take a chance. I'd risk it, to be with him.

But I have to think of Lindsay. My dearest love. The most precious thing in my life. I have to protect her, no matter what sacrifice I have to make. I can't risk being caught and leaving her an orphan. She needs me. Always.

"Ben…I have strong feelings for you. I really do. But I've thought about it and…even though last night was wonderful, I can't have a relationship with you. It's better to just stop now. Before either of us gets hurt."

He looked as if he didn't quite believe she was serious. His eyes narrowed, searching her expression for some clue she might be fooling with him, though it certainly would have been a cruel joke to play.

"I don't understand. You're staying here. You're not leaving. Last night was great… What's the problem?"

Carey bit her lip. This was so hard. It was hard to convince him of something she didn't really feel.

"I… I am going to stay. At least, for a while. But it won't be forever. My life is at loose ends, Ben. I really can't get involved right now. With anyone. Even you. Please try to understand…"

He stood up and walked over to the counter. "Is it because of your husband? Are you still mourning him?"

She sighed. He was offering her an easy out. How simple it would be to just nod and agree. But she had already told him so many lies. He didn't deserve any more.

"No…not really. That's not why." She sighed and shook her head. "The other night, you told me you were looking for someone you could just be happy with. Someone you could make a life together with. Well…I'm not that person. I'm not the person you think I am. I'm doing you a favor, Ben. Just try to believe me."

She caught herself. She was telling more than she'd planned. More than was wise. He looked so confused, so stunned. She wanted to reach out, take him in her arms and comfort him.

She wanted to tell him everything. About the men who were chasing her. The mess her life was in. She imagined him holding her, promising to help her. To protect her.

But what if he didn't?

What if the law officer in him won out and instead, he wanted to take her back to Cleveland, to be a witness at Quinn's trial? Or worse than that, didn't believe that she had nothing to do with Quinn's financial schemes?

Carey knew she just couldn't take that chance.

He stared at her and didn't answer. She saw something in his expression shift, moving past the point of arguing with her anymore. His gaze grew cold and blank.

"You had me going there for a while. The way you acted last night… I can't say I saw this coming."

His words stung. She met his gaze for a moment, then looked away. He made it sound as if she'd used him. Or put on some sort of act, when in fact, it had been just the opposite. Last night was the most emotionally honest time she'd ever spent with a man.

What was the sense in telling him that? He wouldn't believe her.

Ben rubbed the back of his neck with his hand. "Okay. You win." He shook his head and grabbed his shirt off the back of the chair. "If that's the way you want it, fine with me. I'll get my stuff and get the hell out of your way."

Carey's vision blurred. She stood up and watched him stalk out of the room. "Ben…please. Please don't be so angry."

He registered no reaction to her words. Just pushed through the swinging doors and disappeared.

She wanted to follow him, but there was nothing more to say. And no way to make this right. No way for him to ever understand her side of it.

They'd had a single, splendid night together.

More than I deserve, she thought. And one I'll cherish for a lifetime.

With the start of the New Year, Carey felt life slipping into a comfortable routine. She agreed to work twenty-five hours a week, paid partly by a salary and partly by her room and board at the inn. Fitting her schedule around Lindsay's naps and sometimes working after the baby went to sleep, it wasn't too hard to put in the required hours each day.

Unlike offices she'd worked at before, the inn was a lively relaxed atmosphere. Carey felt she was always learning something new and useful. There were always interesting people to deal with and problems to solve. She also liked working with Thea and Luanne Martin. They had both become friends. And Walter Flynn, another important member of the circle.

Ironically, the only family member who she now didn't get along with was Ben.

She knew that he called Thea from time to time. Thea either mentioned it, or Carey overheard snippets of their conversations. But over a week passed and he didn't come by. She suspected he was purposely avoiding the place because of her. The possibility saddened her. She'd never wanted to hurt him. Anything but.

She'd been worried about keeping her distance from him if she stayed on here. She'd never imagined the opposite. That he would purposely avoid her. To the point where she would hunger for the mere sight of him, the sound of his voice.

Over a week had passed—ten days precisely, not that Carey had been counting—when she heard Thea talking to him on the phone and finally worked up the nerve to ask about him.

Carey was inputting invoices from food suppliers. She kept her eyes on the screen as she tapped away on the keyboard. "So, how is Ben? He must be very busy. He hasn't stopped by for a few days now."

Thea was working at her desk and glanced over briefly before she answered. "Oh, Ben never stops by here much. He leads his own life. He'll come once in a great while to fix things. If I complain enough to him. He was just coming to see you. Didn't you know that?"

The honest answer made Carey's breath catch. And made her feel even sadder for what she'd given up. "No...I didn't."

Thea sat back and looked at her over the edge of her reading glasses. "Ben was hurt badly by his ex-wife. Maybe he told you something about that?"

"Yes. He did."

"He hasn't been involved with anyone seriously since. But when I saw the two of you together on Christmas Day, when he brought you here... Well...even before that probably. The way he talked about you on the phone that morning…I must admit, I started to hope. I'm his mother. I'd like to see him happy again."

Carey swallowed hard. "I understand."

"Forgive me, Carey. I know I'm being too intrusive now. But I had the impression you and Ben liked each other. I thought things were…coming along. Now he's run away again. Brooding." Thea shook her head. "Please have some patience with him. He's a good man. But he can be difficult."

Carey realized that Thea put the blame on Ben. When in fact, the reason things weren't going any further between them was all her fault. She waited for Thea to finish, so she could explain.

"I'd like to see Ben happy again. In love. Settling down with a nice woman and having a real life. Maybe he would understand that you can find love more than once in a lifetime. Maybe he would start to accept Walter and wouldn't begrudge me my own happiness."

"I understand. But please don't blame Ben. We do have feelings for each other," Carey admitted quietly. "But I'm the one who broke it off. I can't give him what he's looking for right now. What he deserves. My life is very…unsettled right now. It's just not a good time for me to get involved with anyone."

Thea looked surprised. She sat back in her chair. "I had no idea. I just assumed it was his fault. I'm sorry," she said sincerely. "I appreciate your honesty, Carey. I know you care for Ben. I can see it," she said. "But if the timing isn't right for you, then you've done the right thing. And I want you to know, I didn't offer you a place here because of him, either. You have a place here as long you want it."

Thea's tone was even and calm, her words spoken sincerely. Carey felt touched by her understanding.

"Now, the reason I was just talking to Ben is that I am planning a family get-together for tomorrow night. A little something to celebrate my birthday. I hope you and Lindsay will come. It would mean a lot to me to have you there."

Carey could tell that Thea really wanted her to accept the invitation and it didn't feel right to refuse. Even if it meant seeing Ben there.

"Of course we'll come. Thank you for including us," Carey said politely.

She could tell from Thea's smile that she'd done the right thing. She would just have to put up a good front facing Ben again. More acting. As if she needed another assignment.

The first time after their angry parting was bound to be the hardest. After that, it would get easier, Carey told herself. Though she didn't really believe it.

Friday night came quickly. The birthday dinner was going to be held in Thea's apartment, which was on the first floor of the inn, toward the rear of the building. Carey had never been inside before and was curious to see the place where Ben had grown up. Luanne was making Thea's favorite dinner and had left her cook in charge of the kitchen, so she could both serve and enjoy it. Carey knocked on the door at precisely seven. She'd dressed carefully, thinking of Ben, and had also dressed Lindsay in one of her cutest outfits, thinking of Thea, who doted on the little girl. She carried two gift bags, one with a present from herself and the other, with a little something she'd picked out from Lindsay.

She heard a deep male voice talking to Thea and heavy footsteps coming to answer the door. She waited, almost breathless.

But when the door swung open it was Walter's smiling face that greeted her. "Carey, right on time. Come in, come in," he welcomed her.

Carey entered and looked around. The private quarters were very spacious with a foyer leading to a living room and a dining room and kitchen beyond that. She saw glass doors that framed a view of a stone patio and garden behind the hotel and also saw a long hallway that she assumed led to the bedrooms.

The decor was much the same as the rest of the hotel, warm and traditional with genuine antique pieces mixed with interesting finds.

Walter led her into the living room and offered her a seat.

A bottle of champagne sat in an icy silver bucket and Walter pulled it out and started working on the cork. "We're going to have a toast. As soon as Ben gets here."

Carey smiled but didn't comment, her mind flooded with images of New Year's Eve and sharing a bottle of champagne with Ben up in her bedroom.

She'd poured the last few sips from her glass over his bare torso and licked it off. Following the trail wherever it led.

It wasn't like her to act so wanton and uninhibited. But being close to Ben, making love with him all night long, brought out a side of her she'd never known.

Later, he did the same to her....

And if she had her way, she'd never look at a bottle of champagne, ever again. It just hurt too much to remember.

Thea emerged from the kitchen, carrying a silver tray with crystal glasses and Luanne was steps behind her, carrying a tray of hors d'oeuvres.

They each greeted her happily and Carey rose to kiss Thea's cheek and wish her a happy birthday.

"Thank you, Carey. I know some people my age start to ignore their birthdays. They're ashamed of getting older. I'm not. I'm proud of my wrinkles," she bragged, though she had few that Carey could see. "I've earned every one. I'm grateful for the days, good and bad. You can't appreciate the sweet without tasting the bitter."

"How true." Walter put his arm around Thea's shoulder and

kissed her cheek. "My girl is a philosopher, too. Did you know that?" he asked Carey.

"I've always suspected it." Carey smiled at the way Walter called Thea "his girl." It was sweet, she thought.

It was sweet to see them so obviously head over heels about each other. But it made her feel wistful and sad for what might have been with Ben.

A knock sounded on the door. It had to be Ben, she thought. As if on cue.

Thea went to answer it and Carey heard his voice at the door. "There you are," Thea said happily. "Come in, come in. We're all waiting for you…"

Carey turned her attention to Lindsay, who sat on the floor playing with soft blocks. She didn't want Ben to walk in and find her just sitting there, staring at the doorway.

He walked in with Thea and greeted Walter and Luanne. Finally, she glanced up and met his gaze. "Hello, Carey," he said quietly.

"Hello, Ben. Nice to see you," she said politely.

She looked at him briefly, then turned back to Lindsay, struggling to hide her reaction.

Dressed in a navy-blue sport coat, light blue shirt and gray tailored pants, he looked stunningly handsome. It was hard not to stare. His hair was combed back smoothly, emphasizing the strong lines of his face. The sight of his freshly shaven cheeks made her hands ache to touch his skin.

His voice, the way he walked, the way he laughed at one of Luanne's teasing jibes. Everything about him instantly stirred her senses and she felt utterly overwhelmed.

She suddenly didn't know how she would make it through the night.

Carey had the panicked thought of making some excuse, of claiming she didn't feel well. Or maybe Lindsay seemed sick. But she knew that it wouldn't be right to disappoint Thea that way. Thea had been so good to her the last few weeks. Carey owed it to her to stay. She had to focus on the real reason she was here and forget about Ben. If that was at all possible....

Walter twisted the bottle of champagne in the ice bucket, making a crackling sound that caught everyone's attention.

Carey saw Ben's expression as his gaze fixed on the dark green bottle and she knew what he was thinking. She could tell from his expression he was remembering the last time he'd sipped champagne, too. Where and with whom.

"Time for a toast. To our guest of honor." Walter had already peeled off the foil and wire and now pushed the cork up until it popped. It flew up and arched across the living room, hitting the ceiling. Everyone made a surprised sound.

"Oh, my. That's a lively bottle," Thea said.

Walter wiped the foam and filled the four crystal flutes on the tray halfway. "That's a sign, dear. You're going to have a good year."

Carey glanced at Ben. He stood with his hands clasped together, forcing a small smile. She could tell he was uncomfortable and she sensed it was doubly hard for him tonight. Hard for him to have her here and because he didn't really like Walter.

After everyone had taken a glass from the tray, they all stood. Carey picked up Lindsay and balanced the baby on her hip.

"To Thea. The most wonderful woman in the world. Warm, wise and witty. You're the light of my life and I wish you good health and all the happiness your heart can hold."

"Hear! Hear!" Luanne clinked her glass to Walter's and then to Thea's. "Well done, Walter. Happy birthday, Mom."

Everyone clinked glasses together. Carey turned to Ben last and he obliged, though they both carefully avoided making eye contact.

"Thank you, everybody. I do feel as if I have a great year ahead of me. In fact, I'm certain of it." Thea turned to Walter and he put his arm around her shoulder.

They exchanged a glance, silently communicating with each other, Carey noticed. Thea cleared her throat and stood up a little taller.

"Walter and I have an announcement. Walter proposed on New Year's Eve and I've accepted. We're engaged to be married."

Thea didn't say why they waited to tell everyone. But she followed Thea's glance to Ben, who looked as if someone had just struck him over the head with a two-by-four. Carey guessed Thea must have been wary of facing him with the news.

"That's wonderful, Mom." Luanne looked surprised, but quickly leaned over and hugged her mother. Then she stepped over to Walter and hugged him, too. "I had a feeling something like this was in the works."

"Congratulations," Ben said stiffly. "I hope you'll be very happy together."

"Thank you, Ben," Walter and Thea said in unison.

He didn't make a move to embrace his mother or shake Walter's outstretched hand. "I'm sorry. I have to get going…"

"Ben?" Thea stared at him. "Going? What do you mean? We're about to have dinner…"

"I'm sorry, Mother. I forgot to tell you. Someone called in sick and I have to get back to work. I was only able to stop by to say hello…and wish you a happy birthday."

He put his glass down on the table. He forced a smile that to Carey looked very grim, then he turned and started for the door.

Thea took a step after him. Walter rested his hand on her arm.

"I can find my way out, Mom. I'll call you tomorrow. Save me a piece of cake."

They stood in stunned silence as the door opened and closed. Ben was gone. Thea let out a long, exasperated sigh. "I knew he wasn't going to jump up and down with joy. But I didn't expect him to just...walk out."

"Maybe someone should go after him. He seemed upset," Luanne said. But instead of running after her brother, she looked over at Carey. They all did.

She did want to go to him. Comfort him. Help him through this difficult moment. But she didn't have the courage.

When she didn't make a move, Luanne untied her apron.

"I'll go," she said.

"No, let me," Carey said. She handed the baby to Thea, whose arms were already stretched out to receive her.

Carey quickly ran to the door and let herself out of the apartment. She guessed Ben must have parked out front and thought she would probably be too late to catch up with him by now.

She quickly walked toward the lobby, her sights fixed on the front door. But just as she passed the check-in desk she saw Ben standing nearby. He hadn't left yet. In fact, he looked in no hurry at all, his hands sunk in his pockets, his back turned toward her as he gazed at an arrangement of old photographs that hung on the wall, not far from the entrance.

Carey approached slowly. She already knew what he was looking at, photographs of his father and grandfather and great-grandfather...all the way back to his great-great-grandfather, who had started the inn.

She walked up to him and stood a few steps away. She didn't speak but waited for him to acknowledge her.

Finally he turned his head. His dark blue gaze met her own.

"Did they send you to come after me?" The idea seemed to amuse him, and that stung her feelings. She struggled not to show her reaction. "You can go back and join the party. It's not as if I didn't expect the happy news, sooner or later."

She lifted her chin, staring him down. "What is it then? You don't like Walter? You don't approve of him?"

Ben shook his head and gazed down for a moment. "What does it matter what I think? This is my mother's decision. It's her life. If she wants to marry a man she hardly knows, who's pushing her to put this place in debt and risk losing everything…what can I do about it?"

Before Carey could answer, he turned back to the photos on the wall. "That's my father. You want to know what he was like? He wasn't a smooth talker. He wasn't always raising his glass to make a toast. He wasn't full of hot air and grandiose ideas. Walter has my mother wrapped around his little finger. She'd jump off a bridge if Walter told her to do it."

Carey sat on the edge of an armchair, watching him. "I think your mother has Walter wrapped around her little finger. I realize they haven't known each other very long. But I'm not sure that makes much difference. I think they're really in love."

Ben shook his head and closed his eyes briefly, as if he didn't even want to hear the word. As if the word made him sick.

"If I had a nickel for everyone in the world who thinks they're in love, then wakes up one morning and figures out they were sadly mistaken, I'd be a very rich man, Carey. I'd be a damned millionaire."

Before she could reply, he turned to her, the bitter note in his voice growing harsher. "And what business do you have, getting involved in all this? I thought your life was at loose ends. I thought you didn't plan to be here very long. Isn't that what you told me? Why did you run out here to find me anyway? All of this…it isn't any of your damned concern."

Carey didn't have any quick comeback to that accusation. He'd used her own words to turn the tables on her. To hurt her. The only answer that came to mind would be laughable to him—I came out here because I care about you.

Because I'm falling in love with you.

Because…I *am* in love with you, Ben.

Her silent thoughts made her sit back in surprise.

She couldn't deny it anymore. The words rang true deep inside. She'd probably known it for days now. Maybe even before they'd spent the night together on New Year's Eve.

The stunning realization made her feel very sad...even hopeless. Here he was, standing just inches away. She could have easily reached out and touched him, drawn him near.

But he was separated from her as if there was a thick glass wall between them. The sheer frustration of seeing him, so near and so unreachable at the same time, made her want to scream. Or simply break down and cry.

He shook his head, as if to clear his thoughts. "I've got to go. Get back to the party. Tell them I'm okay."

"All right." She stood up and straightened out her skirt, then caught him looking at her. His beautiful blue eyes looked sad and wounded, and hungry for her.

He stood for a long moment, looking down at her with such longing, her soul trembled.

Then he caught himself and stepped back. He turned and headed for the door.

He didn't say good-night and she didn't call after him.

She knew he wouldn't answer.

Chapter Ten

After the drama at Thea's birthday, Carey did not expect Ben to drop by the inn, or even call. Several days passed before Luanne or Thea mentioned him.

One morning nearly a week after the party, Carey admired a silver bracelet Thea was wearing.

"Ben gave that to me. For my birthday." Thea's tone was smooth and calm, giving no hint of the breach with her son. "He has good taste, don't you think?"

Carey only nodded.

Thea looked quietly amused. "Don't worry. He'll come around. That's why Walter and I planned a long engagement. It might take a while for Ben to thaw out," she added. "Maybe sometime…around spring."

Spring?

Carey hoped he didn't take that long. She certainly wouldn't be here by then.

"When Ben was a boy he once held his breath until he actually turned blue." Thea laughed. "Can you imagine that?"

The problem was, Carey could. She couldn't imagine anyone more stubborn, though, or more determined to stay stuck in his own point of view.

Later that day, Carey noticed Thea making a list of repairs needed around the inn and she felt a spark of hope. That was the list she always gave to Ben. It wouldn't be too long before she saw him, she thought.

But in the afternoon, she heard Thea on the phone, going over the list with Walter. The next morning, Walter arrived, dressed in work clothes. Carey passed him coming in as she took Lindsay out for a walk in her stroller. She'd only seen Walter looking very dapper in finely tailored suits and sport jackets. She hardly recognized him. She had no idea he knew how to unplug a drain or fix a faulty light switch.

It appeared that Ben had been replaced.

Out in the village, she called Paul from her cell phone while she sat in a café with a cup of cappuccino. She'd been checking in with him every few days and so far, his advice was the same. "Stay where you are. It seems the best bet for now."

"Hello, Paul. It's me, Carey," she greeted him.

"Hello, Sunny," he replied, giving her the signal that he was not alone. "Everything okay in Greenland? Still staying warm and cozy, I hope."

Greenland was his nickname for Greenbriar.

"Everything is fine. But I'm worried. I've been here almost a month now. That's too long in one place. Someone is sure to find me…"

"I wouldn't worry about your friend," he said, meaning Quinn. "He's got a lot on his plate right now. Those hunting dogs he had? I think he let them go. Not enough time or money…and they weren't making him happy."

Carey knew Paul meant Quinn was too bogged down by his legal problems to focus on her. That was good news. The hunting dogs had to be the investigators he'd hired.

"He's called off the private investigators?" Carey asked.

"That's what I hear. I don't know about those other dogs, though. The police dogs? They might still be sniffing around."

The district attorney's office, putting together the trial against Quinn.

"So it's still best to stay up here, you think?"

"Greenland seems to be under the radar. You know I'd call you first thing, if I heard any news. The show might have to go on without you, Sunny."

He meant the trial. The prosecutors might give up counting on her as a witness and build the trial against Quinn without her testimony. That would be a miracle, Carey thought. If the trial proceeded and Quinn was found guilty and sent to jail…she'd be free.

Free to tell Ben the truth about herself. Everything.

Free to be with him, if he still wanted her.

Carey would barely allow herself to imagine it.

"Have they set a date for the trial yet?"

"I hear March or maybe April. Our friend keeps asking for more time to rehearse for his performance."

March or April? That was two or three months from now. She couldn't wait in Greenbriar that long. It was too dangerous.

"Paul…I'm afraid. That's too long. I need to keep going. Up to Canada. Like I planned."

"You'll never get through customs," he whispered. "Just take it day by day. Hang in there. Think of Lindsay."

Carey sighed. At least she had Lindsay. Her joy. Her only reason for living these days. Lindsay needed her. Carey was all she had in the entire world.

Paul was right. She couldn't do anything to risk getting caught and being separated from her baby.

Carey returned to the inn feeling anxious and confused. As she walked through the lobby, a flurry of activity drew her attention from her dark thoughts. It seemed that not only had Walter arrived to take care of the minor repairs around the place, he and Thea were starting the renovations, carrying ladders and other supplies upstairs. Closing off an entire section of the hotel so that the rooms could be prepared for redecorating.

It was exciting and a bit frightening. Carey had seen the costs of the project while helping Thea settle on ideas for new furnishings, draperies and wall coverings. Everything seemed so expensive. Ben's concerns about the inn's future with Walter and Thea at the helm didn't seem so far-fetched, or coming only from his negative feelings about Walter.

Carey wasn't sure how Thea was paying for all of it. She hoped with all her heart the ambitious plan was sound and that it would all work out in the end.

Not that she'd be around for Act Three.

The week before, Carey set up a baby monitor so that Lindsay could nap upstairs in their room while she was down in the office. She put Lindsay to sleep in her crib, then went down to the office and turned on the receiver.

"Look at this machine Walter rented," Thea said, showing Carey a huge piece of equipment that took up most of the floor space between their desks. "They just delivered it. It shoots out steam from this side and takes off the old wallpaper. Well, a person has to work it. It doesn't do the job all by itself, unfortunately."

"It's…impressive. Did you hire someone to run it?"

"Walter knows how to work it. He's good at that sort of thing. He's going to do most of that himself. It will save a lot of money."

It sounded like a hot, nasty job and Walter was more than a good sport to take it on, Carey thought.

"What about his own work? Is he taking a vacation?"

"This is the slow time of year for real estate. Especially up here. He can handle most everything over the phone. That's the beauty of being the boss, I guess."

Carey wouldn't know. She'd always been the worker bee.

Still, she thought it was nice of Walter to devote himself to Thea's project so completely. Even though they were engaged, he didn't have to. She doubted Ben knew about this aspect of Walter's involvement.

Carey's help managing the office and front desk was needed more than ever. It wasn't that Thea was doing any of the hands-on work, but it was a huge distraction. At least at this phase.

Thea was like a drop of water, dancing on a hot griddle, Carey thought. She kept running from the front desk or office, up to where Walter was working. Either checking on the progress, or bringing something he needed.

At the same time, Thea was busy drumming up more business for the winter season. Greenbriar was not near any of the major ski areas and only drew a small number of winter athletes, snow-shoers and cross-country ski buffs mostly. Or folks who just liked to cozy up to a roaring fire when the snow piled up outside.

"We have to make this negative a positive," Walter had declared. "If you have a lemon…make a meringue pie. So we don't attract downhill skiers. That leaves all the sensible folks who hate standing out in the cold all day. Antique collectors, wine connoisseurs, people who want to sit by a fire with a good mystery novel…"

Thea had Carey make up special postcards for the inn's mailing list, advertising winter weekend specials—Wine Tasters Weekend, Antique Road Show, Murder Mystery Weekend…

Their plans were ambitious, but creative, Carey thought. She was almost glad Ben wasn't around to criticize their attempts to build up business. She was sure she knew what he would say, calling the ideas cheap and gimmicky.

Carey could see both sides of the argument. She did think a few "gimmicks" were worth a try, though, like Ben, she would hate to see the traditional atmosphere at the beautiful old inn give way to the promotions entirely.

This week, Thea wanted to send out a special letter to the mailing list, advertising a Valentine's Day package—two nights with a gourmet dinner and breakfast, served in the room by request, roses, chocolates, discounts for a horse-drawn sleigh ride through the woods and a visit to the local day spa.

Carey thought the sleigh ride sounded very romantic. As she worked on the description, she imagined herself and Ben, gliding through the snowy woods on a moonlit night, hugging each other close under a heavy throw, the sound of the sleigh bells and the sight of the sparkling stars above.

After the ride, they'd go back to Ben's house. They would sit by the fire and they would…

The phone rang, interrupting her reverie. "Greenbriar Inn, may I help you?"

"Is that your job now, answering the telephone?"

It was Ben. Her heart jumped at the sound of his voice. Caught in her fantasy, her face flushed. She was glad he couldn't see.

"Who's calling please?" Her tone was brisk, businesslike, though she was half teasing him.

"You know damn well who this is. Is my mother around?"

"She's not available right now. Can I take a message?"

"Tell her I finally got in touch with someone who fixes copper gutters. He's coming tomorrow to give an estimate."

Carey made a note. "All right. But I think Walter is taking care of that."

Carey had heard Walter and Thea talking about the leaky gutter yesterday, when Thea had made up the list she usually gave to Ben.

"Walter's doing it, by himself? You can't reach that pipe

without an extension ladder and a scaffold…and a trapeze. The metal needs be patched with a blowtorch."

"I'm pretty sure he's handling it. But I'll tell your mother you called the repairman."

He didn't reply. She heard him breathe out a long sigh. Was he relieved that Walter was so involved now, taking care of the inn's upkeep…or did he feel pushed aside?

Perhaps a bit of both.

"Okay, please do. Thank you." He matched her officious, impersonal tone.

No one overhearing them would have ever guessed the intimacy they'd shared, Carey thought. The way they had lost themselves in each other's arms.

"So, you're getting good at this innkeeper's job. Too bad you're not sticking around. My mother will miss you."

"I'll miss her, too…" I already miss you, she wanted to add. "But I'm not leaving quite yet."

"It's still just a matter of time, though, right?"

She swallowed. "That's right. My plans haven't changed."

It hurt to say that. She wished with all her heart it could be different. Ben still sounded hurt and angry with her, but she sensed he still held on to a slim hope for them, somewhere buried deep in his heart.

"Well, have a good day," he said with mock cheer. "I've got to go."

"Goodbye, Ben." Carey was unable to hide the sorrow in her voice. But he had already hung up, she thought, and didn't hear her.

The large double room Carey had been staying in was one of the first Thea wanted to redecorate. She and Walter thought it was one of the most romantic rooms at the inn and hoped to have it ready for the Valentine's Day Weekend, which was less than a month away.

Thea offered Carey a comfortable but smaller room on the first floor, not far from her own apartment. Carey didn't mind. She had often suggested to Thea that she move, but Thea kept putting it off.

Carey was actually glad to finally move out of the suite. She hoped sleeping in another bed, one she hadn't shared with Ben, would help her not to think of him each night while she tossed and turned.

It didn't help. Not one bit.

The second night staying in the new room, Carey had fallen into a fitful sleep. She woke from a disturbing dream, not at all unusual. But this dream was different from her usual nightmares of being pursued by shadowy, faceless enemies. The dream had been about Ben. He cried out to her, in pain. He needed her help and she couldn't reach him in time.

She woke breathless, her heart racing. It had felt so real. She picked up the clock on the nightstand. It was half past two in the morning. Ben was very likely asleep, snug in his bed in the log cabin, with Dixie curled at his feet.

Or perhaps some other female company. There are other attractive women in the world besides me. Ben wouldn't stay lonely too long, she guessed. She felt a bitter twinge of jealousy toward any women who would share Ben's bed.

Carey rose and checked Lindsay, who was sleeping soundly. She considered going into the kitchen to make a cup of tea, then decided to just settle back under the covers. She felt shaken by the dream and had barely drifted off again when she heard the phone ring next door, in Thea's apartment.

It rang several times, then stopped. A few minutes later, she heard a knock on her door. She ran to open it.

Thea stood there, pale as snow. She was dressed, Carey noticed, but haphazardly. Her hair was uncombed and she was not wearing a drop of makeup. She could hardly speak.

"Thea? What's wrong?"

She gripped Carey's arm. "Ben. He's been shot. He's at the hospital. Luanne and I are going to him. I thought you should know."

Carey felt stunned. She felt all the wind knocked out of her body, as if someone had punched her in the stomach.

Her eyes filled with tears. "Is he all right? Is he conscious?"

"One bullet grazed his shoulder and another hit his leg. He's gone into surgery. They said he's doing all right and should be out soon."

Carey swallowed back her tears. "Let me come with you. Please."

She couldn't stand the idea of waiting alone for someone to call and tell her what was happening. She wasn't family, of course. But she hoped Thea could understand.

"Of course, dear. Get dressed. We'll wait for you." Thea touched her arm lightly. "He'll be okay, don't worry."

Carey nodded. I should be comforting Ben's mother, not the other way around, she thought. But Thea seemed to understand all about her true feelings for Ben. Understand...and sympathize.

Carey readied herself and Lindsay quickly, not knowing how long they might be waiting at the hospital. She tossed all kinds of supplies into the baby bag and hoped she was bringing along the right things.

It was pitch-black outside and eerily silent when Carey carried Lindsay down to Thea's SUV. Luanne was sitting behind the wheel. She'd already warmed up the vehicle and put Lindsay's car seat in the back. Thea sat up front, next to her daughter, and Carey climbed in the back with the baby.

The three women never lacked for conversation at the inn, but the ride was practically silent, each lost in their own thoughts and concerns about Ben.

Carey knew she would give practically anything if he would be all right. That's all she cared about. She didn't care if he never wanted to see her or speak to her ever again. That would be all right. As long as he was okay.

At the hospital, Luanne spoke to a nurse at the admissions desk. Ben was out of his operation and had been moved to a recovery care unit on the third floor.

He was only allowed one visitor at a time and only immediate family, but the nurse in charge allowed Thea and Luanne to go in to him together.

"Just five minutes, please. No longer. He's still under sedation. I don't think he'll even know you're there."

"That's all right. I just need to see him," Thea said.

That was just how Carey felt, too. But she waited in the visitors' area. She wasn't immediate family and didn't expect to see him tonight. At least she could hear how he was recovering.

While she sat in a hard plastic chair, with Lindsay sleeping on her shoulder, a young man in a policeman's uniform arrived. She recognized the Greenbriar Police Department badge, the same one Ben wore.

"Are you here to see Ben Martin?" she asked.

"How's he doing? Hear anything?"

"He's out of surgery, but not conscious yet. His mother and sister are visiting with him now. The nurse said only immediate family tonight."

"I'll wait. They usually let a fellow officer in. I heard about the shooting over the radio. I came over as soon as my shift got off. Ben is one lucky son of a gun. He could have been killed."

"What happened exactly? Who shot him?"

The dangerous side of Ben's job scared her. She never wanted to think about it. But now she felt compelled to hear all the details, to picture how it had all happened.

Ben's buddy told her the story. A call had gone out on the radio about a holdup at convenience store.

"Ben's shift was over. He was on his way home. He didn't really have to go. He wasn't even in uniform."

Carey sighed. Ben seemed to do his best work when his shift was over…out of uniform.

There were two armed men inside, the officer told her, a teenage store clerk and a customer held at gunpoint.

"He was first on the scene but didn't wait for backup."

Somehow Ben got inside through a back door and disarmed one of the gunmen. The second opened fire and tried to kill the clerk, but Ben shoved the boy aside and blocked the shot with his own body. The gunman just missed, grazing Ben in the shoulder.

"He chased the guy on foot and was shot again, but finally fired back from the ground and stopped the dude in his tracks."

Had he killed him? The other office didn't say and Carey didn't ask. The story was violent enough. Perhaps Ben would tell her at some point.

These two gunmen turned out to be known criminals, wanted for a string of jewelry store holdups.

"Ben Martin has ice water in his veins. He's one brave son of a… He's a brave man. A real hero," his buddy said.

Carey nodded and swallowed hard. The story upset her. Ben could have easily been killed. Thea could have woken her up a short time ago with news that Ben was dead and they needed to plan a funeral.

Carey sighed and touched her hand to her forehead, feeling a little faint. "Hey, are you all right? Can I get you some water or something, ma'am?"

"I'm okay. Thanks." Carey struggled to clear her head and sit up again.

"So, you must be his wife. I didn't even know Ben was married."

"He's not… I mean, I'm not his wife…"

The question flustered her. Didn't she wish it?

Thea and Luanne appeared. Carey was eager to hear what they had to say.

"He's still asleep," Luanne reported. "They're not sure when the anesthesia will wear off. He'll be in a lot of pain. But his color is good. He seems to have come through it fine."

Carey's body sagged with relief.

"The nurse said Ben's doctor is on this floor somewhere, at the administration desk. I'd better go find him before he leaves," Thea said.

"I'll go with you." Luanne turned to follow her mother. Then she turned back to Carey.

"You can go in if you like, Carey. It's all right."

"Oh…thank you." Carey rose and slung the baby bag over her shoulder.

Luanne stepped closer. "Here, let me take Lindsay for a while. I'm not sure if they'll allow a baby back there."

Carey thanked her and handed her the baby. Lindsay was so sleepy, having been roused in the middle of the night. Carey knew she'd be no problem at all.

Carey walked back to Ben's room. Luanne had told her where to find him. The room was dimly lit and Ben was connected by wires and tubes to a mass of machinery.

He lay in bed with eyes closed, a bruised, bandaged mess. Carey had never seen anyone look so good to her.

She stepped over to the bed and gently rested her hand on his forearm, yearning to feel his warm skin under her hand. Relieved to reassure herself he was still alive.

She stood that way for several moments, her thoughts wandering, thinking of the moment she'd first met him, all the days in between. The single, magical night she'd spent in his arms. She didn't even notice that his eyes had opened.

When she finally did, he was staring at her. He looked as if he didn't believe she was really there.

He licked his dry lips. His voice came out in a hoarse croak. "Carey?"

She quickly gripped his hand and leaned closer, so she could hear him. "Yes, Ben. I'm right here."

"Thank God." He closed his eyes a moment and rested his head back on the pillow. When he looked at her again, his gaze was filled with tenderness. A look she hadn't seen in a long time.

He gripped her hand, looking eager to tell her something. "I've been a jackass, Carey. I've been so…awful to you. Can you forgive me?"

"Of course I can. I've been mean to you, too. We don't need to talk about it now. As long as you're all right."

He let out a harsh breath. "No…listen. I need to talk to you. To everyone. I was thinking, just when that guy hit me and I fell. I thought, 'This is it. My life is over.' And what a fool I'd been. Life is too short, Carey. Too short to hold grudges, to stay angry at people you love. To push them away…"

Did he really love her? Is that what he was saying? The possibility stole her breath away.

Her throat grew tight and she could barely speak. "Yes, Ben…that's very true."

"I don't care how long you'll be here. I don't care if you're leaving tomorrow, or the next day. Or next year. I don't care how messed up your life is right now. I need to be close to you again, Carey. On any terms. Today is all we have," he pointed out. "Just this moment."

Carey's every defense melted with his words. She felt tears run down the corners of her eyes and wiped them away with the back of her hand.

"I want to be with you, too. I've always felt that way… I just never want to hurt you. That's why I said it wouldn't work."

"I know. But I couldn't hurt any worse than I do now, wanting you. I need to be with you. For however long that will be."

Carey stared down at him. He looked so beautiful to her, his brilliant blue gaze locked with her own. He lifted his good arm and pulled her even closer. She kissed his mouth, softly at first, fearful of hurting him. But he didn't seem in the least bit of pain as he deepened the embrace, pulling her down on top of him, kissing with his whole heart and soul, the touch of his lips on hers, so warm and persuasive.

It was so good to feel his hard body under her, to have her head rest against the same pillow. Carey had been so afraid she'd never see him alive again.

"I guess that's a yes?" he asked as they parted.

She nodded. "I love you," she nearly said aloud.

Instead, her eyes filled with tears and she couldn't stop them this time from spilling over. She bowed her head, resting it on his shoulder. She felt his hand softly stroke her hair.

"Hey, you…don't cry. The worst is over. It's all good, from now on. I promise you."

If only that were true. If only…

She sighed and kissed him again.

He was right. Anything could happen. All they really had was today, this very moment. Didn't tonight prove it? She had to be with him, come what may.

Carey heard someone enter the room. She pulled away from Ben and stood, expecting to see a nurse coming to chase her out.

It was Thea and Luanne. Neither looked surprised, she noticed, to have found Ben and Carey in a close embrace.

"Ben…thank God you're all right." His mother walked over and stood at the opposite side of the bed. "When they called me tonight, I just…"

She didn't finish the sentence. She touched his forehead

with her hand. "There's a police officer out there waiting to see you. He says you were a real hero. You saved someone's life."

"I just did my job. Any other guy in the squad would have done the same."

He looked away for a moment, his expression grim. Carey guessed the shoot-out had been traumatic for him, no matter how he tried to make light of it.

"We spoke with the doctor." Luanne stood next to Carey, smiling down at her brother. "He thinks they'll send you home in two or three days. Isn't that great?"

"But you'll be a long time recuperating," Thea warned him. "I want you to stay at the inn, where we can take care of you."

"I can go back to my place. I'll be all right."

"You will be all right. Eventually. But you've been shot, get it?" Luanne asked him. Her tone was tart, brother to sister.

Thea lifted her chin. "Honestly, Ben. You'll need some help. Just to do the simple things…like take a shower."

The corners of his mouth turned up a notch. Not quite a smile but close enough for Carey to guess what he was thinking. She wouldn't have hesitated an instant to volunteer her help in that department if his mother and sister had not been standing there.

"All right. I'll think about it. Let me get out of here first."

Thea seemed satisfied. She reached out and covered his hand with her own. "You've made yourself scarce the last few weeks, Ben. Now we'll get to make up for it."

Carey met his gaze and held it. They had a lot of lost time to make up for, too.

Chapter Eleven

Ben needed to stay in the hospital longer than his doctors had first predicted. His injuries were painful and serious, though he would never admit it.

After several sessions of Thea's coaxing and logical arguments, he finally gave in and agreed to come back to the inn while he recuperated.

"Maybe for a few days," he said, though Carey expected he would need help for much longer.

They prepared for his homecoming as if he'd been away in the army, on a battlefield. In a way, he had been, Carey thought. They were all so grateful they hadn't lost him and that he wasn't seriously hurt. Thea even made a banner and hung it out over the front porch. Welcome Home Ben.

All renovations were postponed for the day and Luanne had been busy making Ben's favorite foods. Even the local newspaper and TV stations called, wanted to cover the hero's homecoming.

Carey suspected Ben would shun the attention, but noticed that his mother didn't ask him. She just agreed to let the reporters come. She didn't want to pass up such wonderful, free publicity for the inn. "And Ben has always been modest," she added.

Thea was very busy getting the place ready for Ben and for the local media, and there were still guests to attend to. The night before Ben was due to be released, Thea asked Carey if she would go pick him up.

"You can use my SUV, of course. Luanne and I are tied up here and I'd rather not ask Walter."

There were obvious reasons for that, though Ben seemed to have made amends with Walter and put aside his reservations about the engagement.

He seemed to have made peace with the world, Carey noticed, and marveled at how something so good could come of such a violent event.

Of course, Carey was happy to be offered this task and the chance to be alone with Ben for the morning, while they checked him out of the hospital and drove home.

"I can watch the baby for you," Thea offered.

Carey was surprised. "That's all right, Thea. I can take her. It won't be any trouble."

"Oh, I know that. She's a peach. But there's a much bigger baby who'll be demanding your attention. You'd better be completely free to focus on him."

Carey smiled, nearly laughing out loud. Thea loved her son but had few illusions about him.

Ben was dressed and waiting for her when she arrived at his room. He was sitting on the edge of his bed, staring at the door. "Thank goodness. What took you so long?"

"I'm sorry, I hit some traffic. When did you get up, at the crack of dawn?"

"I'm just eager to get out of here. Sorry."

She'd brought along an empty suitcase. She opened it on the bottom of the bed and started packing his clothing and belongings. He silently watched as she folded pajamas and zipped up the toiletry bag.

"Come here a second," he said quietly. Before she could answer, he took hold of her hand with his good arm and tugged her closer.

She took one look at his expression and knew what he wanted. He pulled her down so she sat close to him. She slipped her arm around his shoulder as he pulled her even closer. "Ben…your arm. Your leg…I don't want to hurt you."

"Nothing hurts. In fact, everything feels good. Everything seems to be in perfect working condition…."

He leaned over quickly and pulled back the curtain that circled his bed. Then held his hand to the back of her head and kissed her, long and deep.

Carey melted against him and moaned into his mouth. They fell sideways onto the bed, holding and kissing each other, their legs dangling off the edge, soon tangling together.

Carey knew it was crazy, but couldn't seem to stop herself. Lost in his embrace, she lost all sense of time and place. Since the night he'd been shot, she hadn't been able to visit him again and had only spoken to him once, over the phone.

The things he'd said after the shooting had changed her world. And yet, as the days passed, she began to doubt that he'd really meant it. To wonder if it had been something he'd said due to the shock of his brush with death.

When she'd walked in the door of the room, just a few minutes earlier, she'd still wondered. Now she knew for sure. He'd really meant it. Every word.

She'd imagined this moment for days. For weeks. Just to be with him again, to hold him. To touch him. To breath in the unique, intoxicating scent of his skin.

They were finally together again. Life didn't get sweeter than this….

The curtain was suddenly yanked back. The rattling sound of the hooks on the rod made them both jump and sit up. Carey pushed her skirt down and fumbled with her sweater.

A stern-looking, gray-haired nurse stared down at them.

"Busted," Ben muttered under his breath.

"That bed is for sick people," the nurse said. "You folks ought to get a room."

Carey cleared her throat and looked down at her lap. She felt as if her mother had just caught her on the living room couch with her high school boyfriend.

Ben's cheeks had turned bright red. But he seemed otherwise composed. "Yes, ma'am. We'll be out of your way in no time. Just packing up."

She handed Ben the clipboard. "Read these forms and sign them. You'll need to leave in a wheelchair, insurance regulations."

He scratched his cheek. Carey could tell he hated that idea. "Yeah, I know."

He started signing. Carey slipped off the bed and began packing again. Finally the nurse left them alone.

"To be continued," Ben whispered. The gleam in his blue eyes gave her goose bumps. "I already have the room reserved. But I didn't have to tell her that. Nosy old bat…"

Carey just laughed.

There was more teasing and laughing on the way back to the inn and the drive went by quickly. Even though he wouldn't admit it—and still claimed to be reluctant to stay with his family—Carey could tell he was secretly looking forward to it.

They drove up to the inn and parked in front. Ben caught sight of the sign and balloons and shook his head in dismay.

"What did she do that for?" he said, referring to his mother. "I wasn't away on the space shuttle."

"The balloons were my idea," Carey admitted. She cleared her throat, thinking this was as good a time as any to tell him the rest. "The *Greenbriar Gazette* called and Channel Nine News. They want to interview you."

He stared at her in disbelief. "Interview me? What for? The story was already in the paper."

"It's not about the story. It's about you. How you saved that boy's life. How you feel now. Coming home… You know."

"No, I don't know. I was just doing my job. I don't have anything special to say… I don't want any part of that."

He opened his car door and grabbed his metal walking cane from the backseat before Carey could help him. Then he slid down and landed with a grunt.

Three reporters and a big man carrying a video camera rushed down the porch stairs to meet him. Carey hadn't even seen them standing out there, waiting. Obviously, neither had Ben.

"Oh…damn." He turned his head and looked to her for help. But there was no way to help him now. No escape. He was trapped.

He'd just have to make the best of being a local celebrity.

"Don't worry, Ben," Carey whispered. "Andy Warhol said everyone will be famous for fifteen minutes. It will be over very soon."

The reporters flocked around Ben for a while, then let Carey help him up the steps and into the inn. Luanne, Walter and Thea were waiting in the lobby and most of the guests were, too, watching from a polite distance. Thea held Lindsay in her arms. She had the little girl in a special outfit and even managed to get a bow in her sweet, wispy hair.

Everyone clapped when Ben came through the entrance. He looked startled and then, embarrassed, shunning the attention.

He really was very modest, Carey realized. It wasn't an act.

Dixie had been rescued from Ben's cabin the night he went into the hospital. The dog had been staying at the inn ever since and Carey had been taking care of her. Dixie even slept in her room.

The dog had missed Ben, though. Carey could tell. Dixie now bounded out from behind the reception desk and jumped up on him, nearly knocking Ben down as she licked his face and any other part of him she could reach with her tongue.

"Down, Dixie. Yes, I know you missed me."

He laughed and petted her head. Lights flashed. A perfect shot for the reporters. Carey stood by Ben's side and helped him get the dog back under control.

Having little choice, Ben sat on one of the small sofas in the lobby and answered a few questions. Thea, Walter and Luanne stood close by, but Carey stepped back, out of the circle. Thea handed her Lindsay and she held the baby balanced on her hip and watched from a safe distance.

Finally, the reporters wanted one more picture. The whole family together. Ben waved her over. "Come on, Carey. Get in the picture with us. Sit right here, next to me."

He slid over to make room for her. Carey shook her head in answer. "It's all right. You can take it without me."

But Ben wouldn't let her off the hook so easily. "Come on. One picture. Please?"

"Carey, please get in the photo. It doesn't seem right without you," Thea said.

When Carey shook her head again, Ben pushed himself up off the sofa. She could see the painful effort in his expression. He grabbed his cane and hobbled over to her. Then slung his arm around her shoulder.

"You just can't take no for answer, can you?" she said loud enough just for him to hear her.

"I like to be near you. Haven't you noticed?"

Carey had her own reasons for avoiding the photograph. She turned her head and closed her eyes, hoping her face would be hard to recognize, if anyone looking for her happened to come across the article.

Which would be highly unlikely, she told herself. And they had taken so many photos, there was only a small chance they would use the one with her in it.

The reporters finally left. The lobby seemed suddenly quiet. Thea leaned over and gave Ben another hug. "Oh, Ben. It's good to have you back."

"It's good to be here," Ben finally admitted.

Ben was tired and needed his medication. Along with his mother and Walter, who carried Ben's bag, Carey helped him to his room. It was on the first floor, a few doors down the hallway from her own.

Carey watched him walk around, peer through the curtains at the view, then stretch out on the big bed with a gigantic sigh.

He was still weak, not at his full strength. The morning's excitement had worn him down. Carey took out several pill bottles from his bag and set them on his bedside table.

"Do you need to take any of these now?" she asked, reading the labels.

"One of those blue ones, please." She guessed it was a pain pill. She hated to see him hurting but could tell from the tight look on his face that he was in some pain from his various injuries.

She found the bottle and went to look for a glass of water.

Thea stood next to Walter. "What do you think of the room? Is it all right? I thought you needed something on the first floor. Near me. And Carey," she added.

"It's just fine, Mom. Very nice."

"Walter and I have started renovating and redecorating. Upstairs. The large rooms first."

"Yes, I heard. Carey told me in the car. Sounds good," he added. Carey could see Thea was relieved, hungry for his approval.

"I hope the noise doesn't disturb you, Ben. You tell me if it's too much," Walter said.

"Don't worry about me. I can sleep through a hurricane."

Thea turned to Walter and smiled. "He can. He's not exaggerating."

Thea patted Ben's leg. "We'll see you later. I've got to get back to work. Luanne went back to the kitchen to get you some lunch. She's making your favorite dinner."

Carey didn't know for sure what that was, but guessed that meat and potatoes were involved.

"That's sweet. I'm really not hungry now, though. I think I just need to rest."

"Yes, you rest. I'll look in on you later." Thea leaned over and kissed his cheek. Then left with Walter.

Carey stepped forward and handed him the pill and a glass of water. She stepped back, but he took her hand. "Sit with me a minute."

She sat down beside him on the bed and held his hand. His eyes were half-closed and his breathing had grown deep.

"Does it hurt a lot?" she asked quietly.

"Not when I look at you. Then I don't feel a thing," he said, a small smile lighting up his handsome face.

Carey couldn't help but smile back. "I'm serious."

"So am I," he said quietly. She could tell from his eyes he was fighting sleep, but the pain pill was working fast. He was just about to fall over the edge, into oblivion.

She leaned over and softly pressed her lips to his. He kissed her back and quietly sighed. "That's even better. If you could bottle that kiss, Carey, we'd make a fortune."

Carey rested her cheek on his chest and he touched her hair.

Who needed money? She already had everything she ever wanted, right here.

Carey split her time between working the front desk and office, and caring for Lindsay and Ben. She did have less time for the office work once Ben arrived, but Thea didn't seem to mind. In fact, she encouraged it.

Ben began working with a physical therapist who came for several hours in the morning. He needed help restoring strength to his arm and leg. It was hard work. Grueling at times. Carey didn't enjoy watching him and thankfully, the therapist didn't want anyone around distracting the patient. Those hours were free for her to work and care for Lindsay.

Even in Ben's condition, he was a big help with the baby. He enjoyed Lindsay's company and liked to play with her, or just watch over her while Carey was working. Since the baby wasn't mobile yet, his help worked out fine.

They began to establish a routine. Ben and Dixie joined Carey and the baby on their daily walk into the village. They were quite a sight, Carey thought, the big dog tethered to the stroller and Ben with his cane, moving slowly but managing a bit more distance each day. His therapist said walking, though difficult, was good for him, and would speed his recovery. Ben liked to hear that. Carey could tell from day one he was a terrible patient and already itching to get back to work.

In fact, some days his goal was the police station. He would go in and visit with his buddies while she did her errands and eventually came back for him.

When they got back, Lindsay had her nap, Ben had his therapy, and Carey took over for Thea for a few hours in the office and at the front desk. In the afternoon, she would visit with him again for a while, or he would wander around the inn, checking on the renovations.

"I can't believe Walter is doing so much of the work himself," he finally admitted to Carey. "I guess I've been replaced."

"I guess so," Carey agreed. "They did need to hire a few people to help him. Though I'm sure when you're fit he'll be happy to have you back."

"But demoted. I won't be the foreman anymore."

She searched his gaze, wondering if it really mattered to him so much. "Yes, I think so. Do you mind so much?"

He took a breath then shook his head. "No, not really. I might want to give up police work and take over the inn someday. But I'm not ready yet. I don't need to make it any harder for them to get this place back in shape and run it well."

Since they were on the subject of Thea and Walter and the renovations, Carey thought there was something else he should know.

"I'm not sure if I'm the one who should tell you this. But I know you've been worried about the cost of all the work and how Thea is going to pay for it." She paused and noticed the interest light in his eyes. "She's not borrowing against the deed on the property. Walter is paying for it."

"Walter? He's loaning her the money?"

Carey shook her head. She'd been working with the business records of the inn for many weeks now. She knew all about their financial arrangements.

"No, it's not a loan. He's paying for everything. Just because…because he loves her and knows how important this place is to her."

Ben looked stunned. His expression was serious and thoughtful. She guessed he was reflecting on how wrong he'd been.

"I never imagined that possibility," he admitted. "I guess I need to have a talk with my mother…and apologize."

"I'm sure she'd like to talk to you about it," Carey said.

"I'm glad my mother has Walter's help. I'm glad my mother has Walter," he said finally.

Carey was glad to hear he'd finally come to that conclusion. And somewhat faster than his mother had predicted.

He turned to her and cupped her cheek with his hand. "Everyone should have one special person in the world. That's a real gift. I can't stand in the way of her happiness. That would be very wrong."

Carey didn't say anything. She covered his hand with her own and dropped a kiss in his palm.

Thea had been right. Once Ben had surrendered to his own feelings, his attitude had softened toward Thea's marriage plans. Toward...everything.

At night, she'd leave her door unlocked and Ben would come into her room. She'd slide to one side and welcome him to her bed, eager for his touch, eager to feel his body curled next to hers. They couldn't make love yet, but his kisses and caresses easily swept her away on waves of sweet ecstasy.

Above all, she cherished his nearness, his strong arm wrapped around her as they slept, his body curled around hers.

They spent every spare minute together and grew closer every day. Carey couldn't help but wonder if she could confide her secrets to him. She thought about it almost constantly, trying to work up the courage. To practice the words she would say in her mind. To find the right moment.

But so far, the right moment had never come. There was always some interruption. Or she would lose her courage and pull back.

Her greatest wish now was that Quinn would go to trial and be sent to prison and she could stay here forever. And she would never have to confess to Ben if she didn't want to.

Less than two weeks after Ben left the hospital, he announced he and Dixie were ready to go home, to his cabin in the woods. He'd basked in all the attention and pampering, Carey thought, but he was essentially a very solitary man and felt most comfortable on his own. When Carey asked him why he felt such urgency to leave, he tried to explain that he missed his own house, his retreat.

The bottom line was, he loved his family, but he needed his space.

"I know they mean well, but I can't hear myself think."

Carey had to smile. She knew exactly what he was saying. She loved his family, too, but at the end of the day, she did relish being alone in her private space with Lindsay.

Most people she knew hated silence. They seemed to be afraid of it. Or it made them nervous. They perceived the quiet as something that needed to be filled in, like a blank spot on a painting.

Carey was a great fan of silence. With all the worries she shouldered, a quiet hour helped her to center herself, to regain some balance and perspective. She'd come to see that she and Ben were very much alike that way.

"I want you to come back with me," he said. They were lying on her bed, drifting off to sleep.

Silvery-white moonlight filtered through the open curtains. She could only see the shadowy outline of Ben's face close to hers on the pillow, his blue eyes, wide and watchful, waiting for her answer.

"To your house, you mean?" He nodded. "To help you get settled in again? Of course I'll help you," she said, answering her own question.

"To stay there, Carey… You and Lindsay. I want you to live there with me."

He ran his hand softly down the length of her arm, gliding over her bare skin till her whole body tingled. The sensation was distracting. Carey could hardly believe what she'd just heard.

Had Ben really asked her to come live with him?

"So…will you?" His soft, deep voice reminded her that she'd never answered.

"Yes…yes, I will. All I could think about when you said you were going back is how much I'd miss you."

He pulled her close, winding his arm around her slim waist, his lips pressed to her hair. "Me, too. I don't want to be away from you. It doesn't feel right."

Carey felt the same, though she was too overwhelmed to say. She knew now that she loved him, with all her heart and soul. She had never told him, though. Every time she tried, it seemed the secrets she kept from him, the ugly lies she'd told, stood between them. For some reason, she didn't feel free to tell him that she loved him until she'd told him the truth about herself.

Carey and Ben packed up the next morning. No one was surprised to hear that Carey was going with him. Thea was clearly happy, making all kinds of helpful suggestions.

"Walter will come over later with a high chair and crib for Lindsay. Oh, and a playpen. You'll need a full set of equipment over there now, too. He might as well bring something for dinner, too. You're not going to have time to cook, moving everything in and unpacking…."

Carey was grateful for her help. It could have been a lot different, she thought. Thea wasn't upset at all about rearranging Carey's work hours at the inn. As usual, Thea was very flexible about her needs. Carey knew Ben's mother had her priorities and uppermost was seeing Ben happy.

When they arrived, the cabin looked even more magical, the setting in the snowy woods even more isolated and pristine than Carey had remembered.

Ben was glad to get back to his own house and hobbled up the steps to unlock the front door, Dixie leaping from the car and at his heels.

Carey took Lindsay from her seat and followed them inside.

Ben stood in the foyer, waiting for her. He slipped his arm around her shoulder and pulled her close.

"It's funny. I always loved coming into this cabin, knowing I was completely alone. I just realized that it would have been awful, walking through that door just now without you. I would have felt so lonely. Like I was missing part of me."

Carey felt the same. How could she ever leave this place? Leave him? It didn't seem possible anymore.

"We're home now, Carey," he said. "You're home, too."

Carey met his gaze. She did feel as if she had come home. More of a home than she'd known since she was a little girl. Because she was with Ben.

She reached up and kissed him. That was all the answer she could give.

Between Walter's delivery of the baby equipment and a huge box of food from Luanne, and a visit from the physical therapist, Carey and Ben found they didn't have a quiet moment alone together until late in the evening.

Carey put Lindsay to sleep and joined Ben in the living room, where he'd built a fire. Their dinner had been warming in the oven and he'd arranged two place settings and a bottle of wine on a low table by the big stone fireplace.

Carey settled on some big pillows that were tossed on the floor. Ben poured out two glasses of wine, handed her her own and lifted his in a toast.

"At the risk of turning into Walter…I'd like to propose a toast. To our first day in this house together. The first of many."

Carey touched her glass to his. His words sounded so sure, so optimistic. She tried to feel the same. She could stay here forever, hidden away. She could be safe here, she told herself. But deep in her heart, she still didn't quite believe it.

"So, how do you like living here…so far, I mean?" He picked up an olive and popped it in his mouth.

"Well, I haven't gotten used to the commuting yet," she teased him in return. "But otherwise, it's fine. It's perfect," she added.

"I always thought this house was perfect. Perfect for me," he qualified. "Now I see it was definitely missing something. You…and Lindsay. Now I have everything I need." He shrugged. "I couldn't ask for more."

His tone was light, but his gaze was serious. She couldn't take her eyes from his, even as he moved closer and slipped his arms around her.

"Are you that happy?" she asked quietly.

"Don't you believe me?" He dropped small kisses on her nose and chin, across her cheeks and eyes. "Let me show you, Carey," he said quietly. "No more talking…"

His mouth moved over hers, his kiss deepening, his passion rising. Carey felt herself respond instantly, her body alive with sensations. She was hungry for him, their dinner quickly forgotten.

As his lips savored hers, his fingers smoothly unbuttoned her blouse. He pushed it back, off her shoulders and his head dipped down, moving over the soft sensitive skin at the valley of her breasts. Her cupped her breasts in his hands, massaging the sensitive tips with his fingers and then his tongue, through the lacy fabric of her bra.

When he finally slipped the straps of her bra down and bared her completely, Carey felt as if she'd already melted into a tingling puddle of sensation. He buried his face between her breasts, his mouth and hands working wild magic on her senses. Her entire body felt liquid, molten, electrified. She fell back against the pile of pillows, with Ben's delicious weight on top of her, his strong thigh wedged between her legs, the welcome pressure stirring even sweeter sensations.

Carey tugged mindlessly at his shirttails, her hands slipping under the soft denim fabric and gliding over his warm skin and hard ridges of muscle. She pulled open the front snaps and pressed her mouth to his chest, savoring the taste of his skin, the way his body shuddered when she ran her tongue over a flat male nipple.

He groaned softly but didn't move away, submitting to the exquisite torture of her seductive, knowing touch. Carey kept her mouth pressed to his chest, her hands moving lower, opening his belt and zipper, and sliding into his pants. He felt hot and rigid in her hand. She touched him in ways she knew would bring him deep pleasure.

As his excitement mounted, so did her own, until she could hardly bear it, the desperate feeling of wanting him inside of her. She pressed her body into his knee, the pressure soothing her. He felt her need and slipped his hand into her jeans, then under the edge of her silky underwear, his fingers stroking her hot, wet feminine core into a state of near madness.

When he suddenly stopped, she nearly groaned with frustration. Her eyes flew open and she saw him shed his pants and underwear in one swift movement, ready to slip on protection. She sat up, surprised. He'd never mentioned he'd gotten the doctor's permission to "carry on normal activity."

"We can make love? Are you sure?"

"Honey, I've never been more sure of anything in my entire life. I'll show you the doctor's note later, okay?"

Before Carey could say another word, Ben yanked off her jeans. They flew down her legs and were tossed across the room, while she flipped back abruptly on the pillows. She'd barely gotten her breath when Ben was on top of her again, the rest of his clothes gone. She wrapped her legs around his slim waist, and lifted her hips, desperate to feel him sink into her velvety heat.

He needed no coaxing and she gasped with the power of their joining. A wildfire seared through her.

She moved with him as he thrust inside her, setting a slow,

masterful rhythm, each movement of his body an indescribable, tantalizing pleasure.

Her brain lit up like a neon sign for an instant, then went beautifully blank. No thoughts. Only intense physical sensations registered on her consciousness. It was as if she'd jumped into the deep end of a crystal blue pool, her senses flooded with pure pleasure.

She could barely stand it any longer and never wanted it to end. He gripped her even tighter, her face tucked into the space between his strong neck and shoulder. His skin felt hot and slick. She moved her hands down his back to his hips, and even lower, urging him deeper and faster, matching his movements effortlessly, as if the boundaries between their bodies had melted away. As if they had merged into one single spirit, one single desire.

Finally, she felt herself reach pleasure's peak; her body arched with sharp, sweet pleasure. She felt electrified, incandescent. She trembled and shook as brilliant lights exploded behind her eyes.

Ben moved inside of her once more, pushing through to his ecstatic release. His body arched up as he groaned with satisfaction. She felt him shudder and shake in her arms. Then he fell against her, and she kissed his face, cherishing the feeling of his body covering hers.

Carey felt as if she never wanted to move a muscle, never wanted the moment to end. She wished there was a magic word, or secret switch that could just freeze time, like a photograph in a frame.

Just as Ben had said, Carey knew she had everything she ever wanted now. More than she'd ever dreamed possible.

It just didn't get any better than this. And though she knew she couldn't have it forever, Carey realized what pure happiness felt like now, and that was more than some people had in a lifetime.

Chapter Twelve

Her days and nights with Ben in his cabin in the woods passed in an idyllic haze. When Carey left to work at the inn, Ben watched over Lindsay. He was healing quickly and was much more mobile—as their nightly sessions of lovemaking proved. He could easily handle the baby and was not only good at it but clearly enjoyed her.

Leaving Ben and Lindsay was hard, even for a few hours. But she'd made a commitment to Thea and couldn't let her down. Business at the inn was brisk. Thea and Walter's advertising schemes were drawing more guests and the inn was booked to capacity for the Valentine's Day Weekend, which was coming up quickly. The older couple was excited and making big plans, going all out for every extra touch.

Carey had a lot do each day and was given even more responsibilities. In a strange way, it was good to get away a bit, and be in a different place, so that she could come back. Every time she returned and drove down the long narrow lane that led to the cabin, Carey felt her heart fill with gratitude and peace.

She would sit in her car a moment and stare out at the little house, believing it was hidden so completely from the world that it was virtually invisible. Enchanted. No one could ever find her here. She felt safe here, protected.

The way she did in Ben's arms. And for the first time in her life, truly and passionately loved.

Carey returned from the inn one night and found a note from Ben. He'd gone to the big hardware store in Highland with Lindsay and would be home soon.

She was glad Ben was gone and relieved that she didn't have to worry about Lindsay right now, either. She'd brought home bags of groceries and was determined to make a nice dinner. A celebration dinner, for Ben.

In a few days, the mayor was going to present him with a medal for his bravery. There would be a ceremony at the Village Hall. Thea had already planned a family dinner at the inn to celebrate, but Carey wanted to have one privately, just the two of them.

If Ben hadn't stopped the holdup and been injured in the process, she realized, they may never have gotten together. They may never have realized how much they loved each other.

It was amazing to her to see how good things could come out of tragedies. This time, especially, since her entire life had been changed.

She wasn't much of a cook and they'd so far survived on take-home meals from the inn and her specialty, ham-and-cheese omelets. Luckily, Ben's favorite fare was a no-brainer for most cooks—red meat, potatoes and salad. Since she wanted to be extra daring, she'd gone for a side dish of string beans and some mushrooms.

Carey had spent a small fortune on lamb chops and been lectured by a local butcher on exactly how to prepare them.

She could do it, she told herself. She could have the whole meal ready by the time Ben got back. It wasn't…rocket science.

She started on the potatoes, which she was eventually going to mash. She cut them up and put them in a pot to boil. Then she washed the green beans and started to cut them up, too. She knew that she only had to cut off one end, but didn't remember which it should be, so she chopped off both. Making each bean rather small, she was surprised to see.

By the time she was done, there was only a portion for one. Just enough for Ben, she decided. She didn't need any beans and had always disliked them as a child.

The beans and potatoes were bubbling away when Carey finally tackled the chops. A bit more complicated, to follow the butcher's recipe, which involved bits of garlic and fresh rosemary.

She wasn't used to the broiler and not sure how close the pan should be. The open flames looked ominous. They seemed too close to the meat but…Ben did seem to like that grilled flavor.

A short time later, with all the dishes in play, Carey was dashing madly around the small kitchen, opening windows, the oven fan going full blast. The pot of potatoes was boiling over, the white foam like volcano lava that erupted under the pot lid. The water in the pot of beans had boiled away, Carey hadn't put in enough. The beans had burned, sticking to the bottom of the pot and sending an acrid, scorched smell through the house.

Ben walked in, a curious, worried look on his face.

He didn't even say hello. "Carey? What's the smell?"

She glanced at him, but didn't answer. She knew she looked a mess and wished she had a minute to clean herself up before he got back.

Her makeup had melted away. She was splattered with food stains, her hair was a wild mess, with strands plastered to her sweaty forehead. She had just opened the oven door to check on the lamb chops. Wild flames and a gust of black smoke poured out. She screamed and slammed the door shut.

The smoke alarm went off, and out in the living room she could hear Lindsay crying in her playpen. Carey ran out to her.

Then Ben ran to the wall near the stove and grabbed the fire extinguisher. By the time Carey returned to the kitchen with the baby, he had successfully smothered the fire with streams of white foam.

All over the lamb chops and the rest of the dinner.

Taking a deep breath, he turned to her. "What the heck happened in here? It looks like…a disaster area."

Carey stared around. She would have been mad at him, but he was totally right. She swallowed hard, then burst out crying.

"I was just trying to cook dinner. For you…as a celebration for your medal," she sobbed. "I mean, how many cheese omelets can you eat?"

He laughed softly and walked over to her. He put his arms around her, encircling both her and the baby in a tender embrace.

"A lot of cheese omelets." He softly kissed her brow, and then her cheek. "I can eat a million, if you're making them for me."

She sniffed, her tears slowly turning to a smile. "You'll never eat a million. You'll get tired of them way before that."

"Never." His voice was very solemn. "I'm addicted to them. I need to eat them for the rest of my life…."

She looked up into his eyes and found him smiling down at her with such tenderness and love it melted her heart.

"Will you marry me, Carey? I love you with all my heart and soul. You must know that by now. I never want to be apart from you, whether you're making us omelets, or setting the kitchen on fire…or lighting up my world with your beautiful smile. Will you be my wife?"

Carey was stunned. She would have fallen if Ben's strong arm wasn't supporting her. He laughed at her reaction and abruptly sat down, pulling her down into his lap, while she still held the baby.

"I'm sorry…did I surprise you?"

She took a breath. "I guess so…"

She glanced at him. He looked so happy, his eyes were shining. Happy and handsome, the face she loved to look at. The man she loved.

Her thoughts flew in all directions. Her first impulse was to throw her arms around his neck and accept his proposal. What more could she ever ask for but to live with Ben and be his wife. To have his children and build a life together?

But the dark shadows that flocked around her closed in, their wings flapping with an ominous sound. She could never do that. She could never marry him. Not unless she told him the truth about herself. And even then…

"Carey? Are you all right?" His expression looked more serious, as if he'd drifted down to earth from the cloud he'd been floating upon.

She rose slowly and set Lindsay in her high chair, then began picking up the mess around the kitchen.

"You surprised me, that's all," she said quietly.

He didn't speak for a moment, just watched her. "That's all you have to say? That's not exactly an answer to the question."

She turned and looked at him. Why did she have to love him so much? So much that it…it hurt sometimes?

She took a step closer and faced him squarely. "That was a beautiful question to ask me and it does deserve an answer. I'm sorry."

She took a deep breath, not daring to look him in the eye as she spoke. "I love you, too. I love you more than I ever thought it was possible to love someone. Except for Lindsay." She sighed and stared down at the floor. "I want to accept your proposal. You don't know how much…but I just can't. Not right now…"

Ben gripped her shoulders, forcing her to look up at him. "Why, Carey? Just tell me. Aren't you happy here? You seem to be. You can't just say you think you might leave someday and you don't want to hurt me. I'm not buying that excuse anymore."

Carey didn't say anything. "I can't tell you why. I want to, but it's just very complicated."

And I'm afraid you won't believe me. I'm afraid you'll turn me in to the police.

She tried to twist away from his hold, but he wouldn't let her. "Carey, what is it you're not telling me? I know there's something. Just be honest with me. I can help you…"

"You can't help me, Ben. I wish you could."

"Is it something in your past? Something you did? I can deal with it. Trust me."

She quickly met his glance. "I didn't do anything wrong. Except maybe put my trust in the wrong person…"

"We've all made that mistake at least once or twice. It doesn't have to be the end of everything. Finding you has taught me that," he said quietly.

She stopped pulling away from him and looked up to meet his gaze. "And finding you has taught me that I can find someone to love who is strong and good. Kind and brave and just plain wonderful…"

Her words trailed off. She paused and ran her tongue over her lips that had suddenly gone dry. Her whole mouth had gone dry while she tried to force herself to tell him her story. Her true story. The mistakes in her past that kept her on the run.

He stared down at her, waiting. Expectant. His expression soft with patience and understanding.

Finally, she just couldn't. She lost her nerve and let the chance slip away.

Instead, she moved forward and kissed him, her arms slipping up around his neck. She kissed him as if it were the last time. As if they'd never be together close and warm like this again.

His arms wound around her waist and he kissed her back, lifting her up off her feet with his embrace.

He pulled away first, pressing his cheek to her hair. "Just promise me you'll think about it. You'll think about confiding in me about your problem, whatever it is, and you'll think about being my wife."

She felt her eyes fill with tears and swallowed hard, trying not to cry. "I will think about it, Ben. I promise," she said softly.

She did think about those questions, day and night. Even when she really didn't want to. But she never came to any conclusions about what to do, how to untangle the vicious knots that bound her heart and soul, that had stolen her future and every chance at happiness.

The next morning, Ben had a doctor's appointment and had to leave early, before Carey was due at the inn. She found him showered and dressed, sitting at the kitchen table with coffee and the newspaper when she came down with Lindsay.

She planned to take Lindsay with her for the day and quickly made the baby's breakfast.

Ben put his coffee mug in the sink and kissed her on the lips. His mouth lingered there a tantalizing moment, tasting of coffee. Then he dropped a kiss on the top of Lindsay's downy head.

"I'd better get going, I'll be late."

"Will he let you know today if you can go back to work?"

"I hope so. The physical therapist says I'm ready. I can't wait. Even a desk job. I need to keep busy. I need something to distract me…besides you."

He grinned at her, a gleam in his eye.

She heard the front door close and then heard his SUV start up and pull away from the cabin.

She felt a now-familiar empty place yawn open, knowing she would miss him all day. But she also felt relieved that he hadn't pressed her this morning for an answer about his marriage proposal.

An answer she still wasn't ready to give.

The phone rang. The caller ID read Greenbriar Inn and she quickly picked it up.

It was Thea. She spoke quickly and sounded flustered. "Good morning, Carey. I'm glad I caught you before you left."

"Hi, Thea, what's up?"

"Well, a gentleman just came in, looking for you. He gave me his card. His name is…Ray Paysen. Do you know him?"

Carey felt a chill; goose bumps rose across her arms. "Um…no. I don't think so. Did he say where he'd come from? What kind of business he's in?"

Carey had a strong suspicion, though still held out a small hope that she was wrong and just panicking.

"He didn't say. I told him you would be coming in later. He said he'd come back." Thea paused.

"Oh…all right." Carey forced herself to sound calm and normal. If the conversation with this man was so mundane, she wasn't sure why Thea had called her.

Then Thea said, "I wouldn't have called you about it, since you are coming here today. But there was something very odd in the exchange. It didn't seem quite right…"

"What is it, Thea? What did he say?"

"Well, he took out the photograph from the newspaper, the one in the article about Ben's homecoming. He pointed to you and asked if I knew you. So of course, I said I did and that you worked here. Then he called you by a different name."

"A different name?" Carey tried to sound puzzled and surprised, but she knew very well what was coming next.

"Yes, he called you Katherine. Katherine Judson. Isn't that

odd? I think he must have you mistaken for someone else. I mean, that newspaper photo is awfully blurry. I'm sure you can straighten it out with him when you see him later."

"Right. I'm sure I can," Carey said quickly.

She felt her entire body break out into a cold sweat. If the man had just been to the inn and left, no telling where he might be now.

He could be right outside her door, watching the house. Waiting for her.

He would have just seen Ben leaving, Carey realized, and he would know that she was all alone.

"Thea? I have to go. Lindsay is getting into something and we're not even dressed. I'll be there as quickly as I can manage," she promised.

"That's all right, dear. I know it's hard enough to get out of the house, no less with the baby. You take your time and drive carefully. Everything is under control over here."

"Okay. Thank you…" Carey spoke quickly. Then she paused and took a breath. "Goodbye, Thea," she said, her voice shaking a bit, only hinting at the wealth of feeling under her words.

Thea didn't notice. Or if she did, she didn't mention it.

"So long, dear. See you later," she said brightly and hung up the phone.

Carey felt as if she might burst into tears. Thea had done so much for her. She'd been so kind and generous. Like a second mother. Carey hated to hurt her this way, disappearing without a word of thanks. She thought to write Thea a note. And leave one for Ben, too.

But she didn't have time. She had to get out. As fast as she could.

She raced around the house, making sure the doors were tightly locked, front and back. Then she grabbed Lindsay and ran upstairs. In the bedroom at the front of the house, she stood behind the curtain and peered outside. She waited and watched carefully. She didn't see any cars waiting on the road to the cabin, or tracks leading into the woods. She didn't see anyone outside. Or any sign that someone had been there.

The brilliant sun and clear blue sky seemed to mock her, claiming there was nothing to be afraid of. That nothing bad could possibly happen on such a picture-perfect day.

But Carey knew better than to trust the beauty of the day. She knew better than to hope for happy endings.

She found a duffel bag in the back of the closet and started to empty all of her belongings and Lindsay's into it, whatever she could grab. She tossed in clothes, shoes and makeup, baby care items and toys, all in a huge jumble, leaving half of it behind.

She splashed her face with water and pulled on some clothes. She didn't bother to dress Lindsay and pulled her snowsuit on right over her pajamas. Then she put her coat on and grabbed her purse.

She somehow managed to carry both the baby and the duffel bag downstairs in one trip. She stood at the door, gathering her nerve. She opened the door slowly, just a crack, then peered outside. Her car was parked right near the door. She scanned the woods around the cabin once again, squinting her eyes against the harsh sunlight and glare from the snow. Not a footprint. Not a broken branch.

She glanced over her shoulder at Dixie, who lay in a regal, relaxed pose on a big square cushion in the kitchen. She stared back at Carey, then rested her head on her paws.

If there had been anyone out here, Dixie would have barked her head off, Carey realized. She suddenly felt safer to venture outside and made a mad dash for her car.

She tossed the bag in and strapped Lindsay in her car seat in record time. Then she jumped into the driver's seat and started the engine.

Tears blurred her eyes as she pulled away from the cabin

and carefully steered the car down the narrow lane that led to the main road.

She remembered the night Ben had brought her here. Her curious feeling at first meeting him, her instant attraction. She'd never dreamed she'd end up staying for so long. Or that she would fall so deeply in love with him.

She'd always known that someday, she would go. But she'd never imagined that she'd be forced to leave behind her very heart and soul.

Ben ran to the inn from his haphazardly parked SUV. Every step sent a searing pain through his wounded leg. Still, he took the porch steps two at a time. His mother stood waiting for him. He'd seen her come out as he pulled up. He guessed she must have been watching for him from the sunroom. She looked nervous and scared.

"Ben, thank God you're here…I didn't mean to alarm you. I didn't know what to do…"

"Calm down, Mother. Just tell me everything. Slowly. From the beginning…"

They went back inside. Ben followed her into the office where they wouldn't be overheard by any guests. Walter was sitting at Carey's desk, working on the computer. He nodded at Ben when he walked in, then looked back at the screen.

Thea took a long breath, then began her story. She told Ben about the man who had come in the morning and showed her the newspaper photo. How he had pointed out Carey and called her by a different name, Katherine Judson.

Ben felt a cold fist settle in his gut, but urged her to go on.

"So I called Carey. She was still at your house, getting ready to come here. I told her about the man who was looking for her and how he had mistaken her for someone else from the photo. That's what I thought had happened," she said, glancing up at Ben.

"And what did she say?" Ben asked.

Thea thought for a moment. "She didn't say anything. One way or the other. She said she was coming soon and hung up." Thea's calm gave way to another wave of apprehension. "That was hours ago. I've called her cell phone a dozen times. It won't even take messages. I'm so worried about her, Ben. And the baby," she said, her voice trembling.

Walter rose and stood behind Thea. He rested his hand on her shoulder. "This man came back, Ben," he added. "He told us he was a private investigator. He wouldn't say who he was working for, but said that Carey…or Katherine Judson…was involved in a crime and is wanted by the police. He's been following her from state to state. He showed us a photograph. Not from the newspaper, an older one. She looked completely different. Different hairstyle, different way of dressing…"

"That doesn't prove anything," Ben said evenly.

Inside he felt stunned. Overwhelmed. As if he was suddenly trapped in a nightmare.

"Did he say where she was wanted? What city? What state?"

Walter glanced at Thea. Their expressions were both blank.

"If he did, I don't remember," Thea said. "He said so much, I wasn't thinking straight."

"He said she was a con woman," Walter continued. "That she was known for tricking innocent people out of money. Stealing from businesses, mainly. He'd been hired by a man who had trusted her and lost a lot of money…."

He didn't say more, just glanced down at Thea.

They all knew what he was thinking. Thea was about as innocent and trusting as people came. Carey had been privy to so much financial information at the inn. Thea had blithely handed over everything—bills, bank account statements, tax returns—glad to be relieved of the job, happy that Carey could put all the records into the computer.

Or so she said.

Ben felt his nerves jump. Could it be? Could this be the secret she'd been hiding from him all these weeks?

He'd imagined all kinds of possibilities—but never this. A grifter. A con artist. An embezzler. Wanted by the police, the P.I. had said.

He felt something deep inside of him crash. Crash and burn.

He stared up at Walter. "Have you found anything missing? Has she stolen any money from here?"

Walter sighed. "I haven't seen anything odd in the books yet…but that doesn't mean a thing. She could have been very good at it. It may take weeks for us to find out."

Ben knew that was true.

"Oh, Ben…I'm so sorry." Thea shook her head, her eyes glassy with unshed tears.

Ben reached out and patted her hand. "It's not your fault, Mom. How could you have known?"

"She seemed so sweet. She made you so happy. I encouraged her to stay here. I thought it was the right thing to do…"

"Thea, you can't blame yourself." Walter put his arm around her shoulder. "We all liked her. She knew how to win us over. How to trick us. That's the way these people operate."

These people. Walter already had her lumped together with the dregs of society. Ben let out a long harsh breath. He felt anger building inside of him and he didn't want to take it out on Walter. Or his mother.

"Where is this man? Did he leave a number?"

"He gave us his card." Thea took the card out of her pocket and handed it to Ben. "That's his cell phone number, down there."

Ben stuck the card in his pocket. He had to get out of there.

"Okay. I'm going down to the station. See if I can figure any of this out. If Carey calls…"

"We'll call you right away. Don't worry," Thea said.

Walter didn't say anything. He left Thea in the office and followed Ben out to the lobby. "It's hardest for you, Ben. I know that. You loved her."

Ben noticed how Walter used the past tense of the word.

"I still love her, Walter. It doesn't just turn off, like a water faucet."

"No…of course not. I'm sorry. It's just such a shock. We know she could be innocent."

"Yes, she could be," Ben agreed.

Walter reached out and rested his hand on Ben's arm for a moment. He gazed up at Ben with a look of sympathy. "What will you do now? Try to find her?"

Ben nodded. "Yes, I guess so. I don't know where to start," he said honestly.

"Can I come with you? Do you want some help?"

Ben was surprised by Walter's offer. Surprised and touched.

He shook his head. "Thanks…that's okay. I'd rather be by myself right now."

"I understand." He nodded. "Call when you can. Let us know how it's going."

"I will," Ben promised. He turned and walked out the door and headed for his car, having no idea where to look first for her, what direction to go in, where she might be headed.

He started his car and drove it around the corner, out of sight of the inn. He parked on a dark street, away from the streetlamp.

Then he put his head in his hands and cried, his body shaking with harsh, choked sobs. He couldn't remember crying like that since his father died. And before that, never.

He felt foolish, stupid, taken in. All that time, she must have been laughing at him. He couldn't say she'd never warned him. The times she'd pushed him away, put him off…that, too, could have been part of her act. One of her ploys.

He'd fallen for all of it.

He wiped his eyes with the back of his hand and shook his head to clear his thoughts.

If she could be found, he would find her. He would hear it from her, who she really was, what she'd done. She couldn't just pick up and run from him. Break his heart. Without a word of explanation.

He wouldn't let her get away from him that easily.

Ben drove for hours, covering a wide stretch of territory with Greenbriar at its center. He stopped at every motel and bed-and-breakfast, service station, and convenience store he passed, describing Carey and Lindsay, her beat-up old car. What they might be wearing.

No one had seen them. No one had even thought they might have seen them. He put out an all points bulletin for her on the police radio and got his commander's permission to send it out through the entire state. Carey was a wanted woman. A woman on the run.

She wouldn't get too far, he told himself. He tried to believe that.

Somewhere in his travels, he called the private investigator, Ray Paysen. He dreaded the call and had put it off for hours, but was still curious to find out if the man had made any progress.

"Paysen," the man answered.

"This is Ben Martin. You spoke with my mother today about Carey Mooreland, at the inn?"

"Oh, Martin. Sure… Have you heard from her?"

"No. We haven't. We wondered if you had any news."

"Not a thing."

There was something about the man's tone Ben didn't like.

He usually had good instincts about these things. Instincts that had helped to keep him alive, through almost fifteen years of working in law enforcement.

"Mr. Paysen, I'd like to ask you a few questions. You say Carey Mooreland is wanted by the police for embezzlement?"

"That's right. She's a con artist. A good one, too."

"And who are you working for? My mother wasn't sure," Ben lied.

"The D.A.'s office. They want her for questioning in a big case."

His mother hadn't mentioned anything like that. Could she have gotten confused? It was possible. She was very distraught by the news.

"What D.A.'s office? There are a lot of them, you know," he joked. "What jurisdiction?"

Paysen didn't answer right away. "Are you a lawyer or something?"

"I'm a cop. Greenbriar Police Force."

"Oh, I see."

Ben wasn't sure what he meant by that. That Ben couldn't be shaken up and confused by double-talk, the way his mother was? And Walter, too, for that matter.

"I was thinking, Mr. Paysen, maybe you should come down to the station tomorrow morning. So we could put our heads together. Share information."

Paysen didn't answer for a moment. "Sure. Good idea. I'm not sure what time I can make it back over there, though. Can I call you tomorrow?"

Ben knew when he was getting the brush-off. The fact that this guy didn't want to meet face-to-face was another red flag.

"Sure thing. You have my number now. On your cell?"

"Right. I'll make sure I don't erase it. And listen, if you hear anything about her at all, you let me know. This is an important case. It will look good for you if you help us bring her in."

"I understand." As if he needed this man's help with his career. They rang off and Ben drove on. The highway was a long black ribbon, curving into the night. Dark and empty, the way he felt inside.

This Paysen called himself a private investigator. But had he ever shown anyone a license? Even if he had, would his mother or Walter even have known if it was real or not?

This morning, the P.I. said he'd been hired by an injured party, a victim of Carey's wiles. Now he claimed he was working for a district attorney's office. Though he still had not said who or where, Ben realized.

Something told him he had to find Carey before this man Paysen did. Something wasn't right with him. Ben could just feel it.

No matter who she really was, or what she'd done, he couldn't turn away from the single surviving truth—he loved her. He still did and always would. He would still do whatever he could to protect her. To help her survive whatever trouble she'd mixed herself up in.

Until he heard the whole story from her, he wasn't going to just believe some stranger's word against hers. He wasn't going to just…give up on her.

Chapter Thirteen

Ben drove all night, until the sun came up. A big circle around the whole state, at least it felt like it. More like a circle around Greenbriar. A circle that turned out to be empty inside.

He couldn't stand the idea of going home to the cabin. But he knew Dixie was waiting there. She couldn't be neglected.

He ended up curling up on the couch in his clothes, an afghan pulled up over his shoulders. He couldn't face the bed he'd shared with Carey.

Or Katherine.

Whatever her real name was…

His exhaustion was a lucky thing. Once he put his head down, it felt as if a black curtain had dropped over his consciousness. He was blessedly relieved of all thoughts. All images of…her.

He woke the next morning, feeling real pain, in the leg and shoulder where he'd been shot. The searing pain in his body was nothing compared to the one in his heart.

He could barely take a breath. But he knew he had to push on.

He sat up and checked his cell phone. One message from the questionable P.I. "Martin? It's Paysen. I'm sorry, man, but I just can't get back your way today. You keep in touch. Let me know if you hear anything. Be talking to you."

Ben was not surprised. The message only underscored his suspicions. He imagined for a moment how scared she must be with this man after her. How frightened and alone. He felt an even stronger urgency now to find her.

Ben showered and dressed in clean clothes, then drank his fill of strong coffee. He spent most of the morning in the police office, working on the computer and making calls. It didn't take long for the entire force—all five of them—to learn of his troubles and the story quickly spread to the police stations in neighboring towns.

Ben was nothing if not a private man. It was hard to reveal his personal crisis—what some would think was total gullibility. A man losing his mind over some woman. He felt humiliated. Especially in front of his fellow police officers.

But he did what he had to do.

Working with police records was harder. The records of one county or state weren't that easily accessible to others. This wasn't the way it should be ideally, but it was the reality.

He worked with a station secretary who knew how to navigate the different information paths. He also didn't have her fingerprints, or social security number. Not even a fake one, to go by. That made it harder to find her, too.

Every hour that Carey Mooreland—or Katherine Judson—failed to turn up on the computer list of wanted criminals, Ben felt secretly cheered. But he knew the process could take days, and it was foolish to be optimistic.

Foolish to believe that she was innocent.

After three solid days of police work—of driving all over

the state, of questioning and showing photographs, of calling in every favor anyone had ever owed him in his life—Ben felt drained and hopeless.

She could have made it to Canada by now. She could have made it to Mexico. If she was that clever a criminal mind, she could have changed her appearance, her identification, her entire personality. She could have simply disappeared into thin air and he would never see her again.

The thought cut like a knife.

Everyone in town knew what had happened to him. His mother had happily spread the news that he and Carey were living together—the beautiful young widow Ben had rescued in the snowstorm on Christmas Eve. That was the way she described it. She expected a wedding soon. Maybe even before her own.

Well, she had almost been right, Ben thought.

Who could have predicted this ending to that fairy-tale romance?

Any day now, he expected a headline in the local paper. Hero Cop Deceived By Con Woman. He would have deserved it, too. What was it about him that made him fall for deceitful women? Women who ended up betraying him? Hurting him?

Eva had betrayed him. But the pain had been nothing compared to this, he realized. No, Carey was different. He'd loved her in a different way altogether. And now he was paying for it, big-time….

Ben had no choice but to sit at a desk in the station. To make calls and wait for calls, hoping some tiny lead would emerge.

He'd never heard from Ray Paysen again, though he called the man daily, trying to keep tabs on him. It was a cat-and-mouse game, he knew. He was hoping Paysen would lead him to Carey and Paysen was hoping the same about him.

Ben was just about to pack it in for the day, when a call came into the station for him. He picked it up and recognized Harry Anderson's voice on the line.

"Harry? What can I do for you?" Ben hadn't needed his car repaired lately and knew that Carey's bill had been paid in full.

Hadn't it?

"Sorry to bother you, Ben. I heard about Carey. Her running away… I just got a call over here. It might be nothing. But I thought I should let you know."

"Yes, what is it?" Harry had his complete attention now.

"A friend of mine owns a station up in Bar Harbor. He called looking for a part. A reconditioned axle for a compact, import. Ten-year-old model."

"And?" Ben didn't get it. What was Harry talking about? What did all this car talk have to do with Carey?

"That's the same model Carey has," Harry said simply. "He described the car, gray body, banged-up in front. Says a woman with a baby brought it in. The axle must have been cracked in the accident. I never realized it. It must have just given out on her…"

"That's all right, Harry. Good thing you missed it." Ben gripped the phone. "What's his name and number, this friend of yours?"

Harry gave Ben the information and he jotted it down. Then he quickly said goodbye and ran out the door.

He drove as quickly as he dared in the cruiser, weaving in and out of traffic on the highway, his lights flashing. But the drive up to Bar Harbor from Greenbriar was still a long distance, several hours.

Calling on his cell phone from his car, he'd managed to catch the mechanic there before he closed the shop. Harry's friend described Carey and Lindsay pretty accurately. Though, according to his report, Carey now had brown hair.

She brought the car in about two nights ago, he recalled.

He also gave Ben the name of the motel where she was staying. Ben prayed to God that she was still there and hadn't moved around overnight to cover her tracks. Bar Harbor was a resort town, and looking for her there would be like looking for a needle in a haystack.

There was a ferry to Nova Scotia in Bar Harbor. He suspected she'd been planning to get on when her car broke down. He hoped she had not decided to just leave the car and go on the ferry without it.

Ben reached Bar Harbor and drove straight to the motel.

It was located outside of town, on a side street. A sign out front read Harbor View though there was no water of any kind to see from this tucked-away corner of town. Unless you counted a Laundromat next door.

Ben went to the office, showed his badge and found out Carey's room number. The desk clerk said he'd seen her go inside a few minutes ago.

Ben walked to the room and knocked. He heard her walk over to see who it was. Then heard her gasp through the thin wooden door.

"Carey…let me in." He waited but she didn't answer. "If you don't let me in, I'll open it with a key."

"Go away, Ben. You shouldn't have followed me."

"I'll break this door down if I have to. Don't try me."

That got her attention, he noticed. He heard the chain lock slide and the latch clicked. She opened the door and stepped back.

Her hair was brown. It startled him. But it wasn't unbecoming. In fact, the darker shade complemented her fair skin and brown eyes.

She looked nervous and ashamed, he thought. Her head was bowed; she wouldn't look at him.

"Why did you come? Are you going to turn me in?"

"That depends," he said honestly. "I need some answers. The truth. Finally. Do you think you can manage that?"

His tone was rough. Harsher than he'd meant it to be, but he couldn't help it. He could see he had frightened her. She shrank back and he felt sorry. But didn't make a move to reassure her.

"How did you find me?" She took a few steps away from him and sat in an armchair.

"That doesn't matter." He waited. She didn't speak. "So? Are you going to talk to me? Who's Katherine Judson?"

"I am. That's my real name."

That hurt. So that part was true. "Why Carey Mooreland? Who's she?"

"Carey is just a nickname my family called me. Mooreland is my mother's maiden name." She took a deep breath. "I wanted to tell you all this, Ben. I wanted to tell you everything. I got scared. I didn't think you'd believe me."

"Tell me now. Let's see. I've heard a lot of stories about you…Katherine. I need to hear your version. You owe me that at least, don't you think?"

She nodded. "Yes, I do."

She glanced at him, then looked straight ahead.

Then she told him the whole story, starting with her husband Tom's death. How Quinn had helped her financially, how he had given her a job in his office after the baby was born. She had been taken in by him, and had at first not realized he had romantic feelings for her. Romantic…delusions.

She told Ben how Quinn fooled around with the bookkeeping and tax records in his company without her knowing and then, when she confronted him, he'd threatened to get her into trouble if she went to the authorities. He'd promised to convince them she had been a party to it. She had been the bookkeeper and handled a lot of financial records. It would have been his word against hers.

She described how angry Quinn got when she ever mentioned finding a new job and moving away. His anger was frightening, crazy. She'd grown scared of what he might do. So she'd run, with the help of friends, Paul and Nora.

She'd first gone to Chicago, which had worked out for a while. But Quinn had investigators on her trail and they had found her. She'd narrowly escaped, traveling next to Vermont, and ending up in Blue Lake. A small town a lot like Greenbriar.

She'd been happy there for a few months, she told Ben, and had made good friends. But on Christmas Eve morning, she'd learned that she'd been discovered once again.

To make matters worse, Quinn was in legal trouble. He'd finally been connected to a ring of businessmen who were defrauding banks of millions with fake mortgages and loans. Carey thought his heavy legal problems would finally distract him from chasing her.

"But the prosecutors investigating the case thought I might have been part of the group. Or at least, had some valuable testimony against him," she concluded.

"So, they're after you, too."

"That's right."

"And you haven't done anything wrong? You haven't defrauded anyone or embezzled money from a business?"

Carey shook her head slowly. "Is that what you heard about me?"

Ben didn't answer. He couldn't. His head was spinning. Was she telling him the truth…finally? Did he dare believe it?

"I can understand why you didn't want to tell me, but why didn't you tell…someone? Why didn't you contact the D.A. and tell your side of the story?"

"I didn't think they'd believe me. Even if they did, they would have made me testify against Quinn. They didn't have a very strong case, I'd heard. Not without me. And if the good guys lost, where would I be? He'd find me faster than you did, no matter where I'd try to hide."

She covered her beautiful face with her hands, then looked back up at him. Her eyes were red rimmed and swollen. It looked as if she'd been crying. Crying a lot, he thought. The way he had been.

"I had to think of Lindsay. That's all I focused on. Protecting her. If anything happened to me, who would take care of her? Who would raise her? I know it wasn't right and I should have helped build the case against him. But I couldn't risk it. I had too much at stake. I had to keep going...."

"Where were you going when I found you? Not to a job in Portland, like you claimed."

"No...there was no friend there. No job." She sighed. "I was on my way to Canada. I thought I could finally shake free of all this up there."

"But you didn't make it."

"No...I didn't." She looked at him again. "Instead, I found you, Ben."

"I was the one who found you," he quietly corrected her.

"And now you've found me again." She waited a moment. "What will you do with me this time? Do you believe me?"

He let out a long shaky breath. "Maybe I'm the biggest fool in the history of mankind...but yes, I do believe you. I want to help you, Carey." He couldn't help calling her that name. He always would. "Will you let me?"

She nodded. "I need your help. I just need you. Period."

"I need you, too. No matter what happens. I know that now."

She stood up and faced him and he took her in his arms. She slipped her arms around his waist and pressed herself to his body.

He felt her shaking. She was crying, her face hidden on his shoulder. He stroked her hair, then lifted her chin and tenderly kissed her lips. Tasting her tears.

Finally, he pulled his head back and looked down at her.

"Any more questions for me?" she asked quietly.

"Have you thought any more about marrying me? You never answered that one."

She stared at him, looking almost as surprised as the first time he'd asked her. "Are you serious?"

"I've never been more serious in my life."

She waited so long to answer him, he steeled himself for another gentle rejection.

"Nothing in the world would make me happier than to be your wife," she said finally. Her quiet words made his battered heart sing. "I love you so much… I'm sorry, Ben. I'm so sorry for what I put you through. Can you forgive me for that?"

"You put me through hell," he admitted. "But somehow, I've forgotten everything. It feels like a bad dream."

It was true. All of the pain and sorrow of the last few days were instantly forgotten once he had Carey back in his arms.

To think, he'd almost given up on her. He'd almost been persuaded that she was someone completely different from the woman he had fallen in love with.

They quickly gathered up Carey's belongings. Lindsay was asleep and needed to be dressed in warm clothes for the ride home. Carey put the baby in her car seat, covered her with a blanket and she fell asleep again.

They were about to leave the room, when Ben asked her to wait. He opened the curtain a crack and glanced out the window.

Then he took out his cell phone and made a call. It sounded as if he was handling police business. Carey couldn't be sure.

"Yes, he's here. A tan sedan. Ohio plates. He's parked at the far end of the lot, near the Dumpster. All right. We'll wait here. Just ring the phone when it's over."

He hung up. "We need to wait here a few minutes before we can leave."

"Why? What's going on?" Carey's pulse went into panic mode again. She was totally exhausted from the last three days and had thought this ordeal was over.

"There was a man following you. He claimed to be a private investigator working for a district attorney. He claimed a lot of things," Ben added. "I had a feeling he was tailing me and had followed me up here. The Bar Harbor police are about to pick him up. Get him out of our way for a while."

Carey sighed with relief. "You're a pretty good policeman, aren't you?"

"The star of the department…though there are only five of us."

She laughed, remembering the joke he'd told her the night they'd met.

She stepped close and put her arms around him.

"I think you're too modest, Ben Martin… I think you're too wonderful to be true."

"I thought the same thing about you. See how wrong I turned to be? You are just as wonderful as you've always seemed to me, Carey…."

He pulled her close again and kissed her as if he'd never let her go.

Minutes later, the ringing cell phone signaled an all clear.

They didn't hear a thing.

Epilogue

Carey sat on a cold marble bench in the courthouse lobby. It was after five o'clock and the building was practically empty. She was glad it was quiet. Her mind needed some rest after the long day. She glanced across the lobby. Ben was still talking with her attorney and the assistant D.A. who had come from Cleveland to question her. She felt so exhausted, she didn't have the energy to join them.

She pulled out her leather gloves and tugged them over her hands. Her gaze lingered on her left hand, on the glistening gold wedding band. She and Ben had been married now a little over a week and seeing her ring still surprised her. She felt so lucky, so blessed. She thought it would always surprise her a little, the way things had worked out for her and Ben. She'd never take anything for granted again.

She and Ben had been married in a quiet, private ceremony

a day after her return. Ben's sister had made a special dinner at the hotel, and his family had celebrated with them.

Carey had felt awkward at first, facing the Martins. She was so sorry for deceiving them. She wondered if they would be able to forgive her. But Thea, Walter and Luanne had welcomed her back warmly, in a way she'd never expected. They felt sorry for ever doubting her, and sympathized with the danger she'd faced and the complicated problems she'd been handling all on her own.

Carey never blamed Ben's family for being tricked by Quinn's private investigator. They were good-hearted, trusting people and had been an easy target for a predator out to deceive them.

Would the district attorney's office working on Quinn's case have treated her differently if she had not been the wife of a law officer? Carey would never be sure, but she was glad she never had to find out. She did know for sure that she could never have gotten through the ordeal of coming forward as a witness without Ben's practical help and loving support every step of the way. As much as she had wanted to do the right thing and help put Quinn away, putting herself and Lindsay in jeopardy had made it seem so impossible to her. But that was not a problem now.

Ben's connections—his friends and friends of friends—had cleared a much smoother path for her than she'd ever been able to manage on her own. Ben had found her a good lawyer, skilled at negotiating with prosecutors for reluctant witnesses. He'd also reached out to fellow officers, who had in turn reached out to their own connections, until they had a contact on Quinn's case in Cleveland, willing to consider Carey's concerns.

More evidence and testimony had been collected. The D.A.'s office knew Carey was not involved in the scheme, though they more or less admitted they would have tried to scare her with that card if they'd ever caught up with her.

Finally, a deal was worked out and Carey was permitted to give a deposition at a courthouse in Vermont, and agreed to go to Ohio for the trial if her presence was deemed necessary.

So here she was, and had been all day. The ordeal had taken several hours. Ben had not been permitted in the room, though she did have a lawyer with her, protecting her rights. It had been a harrowing, exhausting experience, partly because so many of the questions forced her to remember a part of her life—and the man—she had tried so hard to forget.

Finally, there were no more questions, and Carey was free to go. She'd practically run out of the room, straight into Ben's open arms. Carey had started crying and couldn't stop. She'd excused herself for a while, and cleaned up in the restroom. When she'd come out, Ben was involved in another conversation with the two attorneys.

She looked over at her husband, feeling their silent, uncanny connection, as if a string stretched from her heart to his, always keeping them close. When she thought back now, from the night of their first meeting to the moment of their marriage vows, she felt as if they'd always been meant for each other. Two halves of a whole that fit together perfectly. When they were apart, she held him in her heart and knew he was part of her.

Finally, she watched the three men shake hands, and Ben came toward her, his blue eyes shining, his smile wide. He looked very dignified in a dark blue suit, white shirt and silk tie. He hadn't even dressed up that formally for their own wedding, she reflected with a smile.

He stood beside her, put his arm around her shoulder and pulled her close. "How do you feel? You must be exhausted."

"I don't know whether to laugh or cry. I'm just so relieved." She looked up at him. "It was the right thing to do, Ben. But I couldn't have done it without you. Thanks," she added quietly.

"Carey...you never have to thank me. You're everything to

me—you and Lindsay. I'd move mountains for you if I could," he promised with a small smile.

Carey smiled back. He'd just helped her move the biggest mountain of her lifetime, one that had been blocking her way for so long. Now she felt free, almost weightless with relief. As if she might float away if he wasn't holding on to her so securely.

"What would you like to do now? Get a bite to eat? I think there's a park across from this building. We could get some fresh air and stretch our legs awhile."

Carey sighed. She twined her fingers in his large, strong hand. "Let's go home."

He met her glance and nodded. His smile still took her breath away.

"No argument here. I wanted to take you home from the first minute I found you."

She knew what he'd said was true. And she was so happy now that he'd done just that.

As he pushed open the heavy door and let her step through, she felt as if she was starting a whole new part of her life. The life they would share forever, together.

* * * * *

Mills & Boon® Special Edition
brings you a sneak preview of

Cathy Gillen Thacker's Hannah's Baby

It is the happiest day of her life when Hannah
brings her adopted baby home to Texas. But
what would make the new mother really happy
is a daddy to complete their instant family. And
Hannah's friend Joe Daugherty would make a
perfect father. He just doesn't know it yet!

Don't miss this exciting new story coming next
month from Mills & Boon® Special Edition,
which is available in July 2009!

Hannah's Baby

by

Cathy Gillen Thacker

Hannah Callahan stood on the porch of her childhood home, savoring the cool breeze of a perfect summer morning, watching dawn streak across the vast mountains. She had grown up in Summit, Texas, and although she had spent most of her post-college years living out of a suitcase in hotels all over the world, she was glad to leave those nomad days behind her. Glad to be starting a new chapter of her life.

A dark-green Land Rover made its way up the quiet residential street.

Hannah acknowledged the driver and wrestled her suitcase down the broad wooden steps of the prairie-style home.

Thirty-five-year-old Joe Daugherty left the motor running and met her halfway up the sidewalk. He was dressed in loose fitting trousers and a vibrant striped shirt that brought out the evergreen hue of his eyes. As always, the sheer size of his rugged six-foot-three frame dwarfed her considerably smaller body.

Hannah shifted her gaze from his broad shoulders, trying not to notice how petite she felt in his presence. She and Joe had met five months earlier. He'd come into the store, and the two of them had hit it off immediately. She'd been instantly and undeniably attracted to the sexy adventurer. He had seemed similarly interested. Had she not been so ready to settle down, and had he planned to stay in the area for more than the six months it took to research and write his book, maybe they would have gotten together. But Hannah was not interested in beginning an affair that would only have to end, so they'd relegated each other to the category of casual friend, nothing more. The fact he was going on this trip with her was a fluke, the kind of favor not likely to be repeated. She needed to remember that.

The emotion simmering inside her this morning had nothing to do with the arresting features of his masculine face, or the way the short strands of his hair gleamed against the suntanned hue of his skin. Nor did it have anything to do with the amount of time she was going to be spending with Joe Daugherty over the next week. Her racing pulse was caused by the continuing tension between her and the only family she had left. Anticipation of the events to come...

Oblivious to her tumultuous thoughts, Joe slipped his strong hand beneath hers to grip the handle on her wheeled twenty-six-inch suitcase. "This all the luggage you've got?"

Hannah nodded around the sudden lump in her throat and clasped the red canvas carryall of important papers and travel necessities closer to her body. "I just need to stop by the Mercantile and say goodbye to my dad." Try one last time to talk some sense into him.

Joe fit her suitcase next to his and shut the tailgate. "No problem." He slid behind the wheel while she jumped in to ride shotgun. He looked over his shoulder as he backed out of the drive. "We've got plenty of time."

But not enough to change her dad's mind. Hannah swallowed, beset by nerves once again. "Thanks for going with me."

Joe shrugged and flashed her a sexy half smile. "Hey. It's

not every day somebody offers me an all expense paid trip to Taiwan."

"Seriously—"

"Seriously." He sent her a brief telling look that spoke volumes about his inherently understanding nature. "You need somebody to accompany you who has a current passport and no fear of the complexities of international travel. Someone who knows that particular region of Asia, not to mention the language, and is footloose and fancy-free enough to be able to drop everything and go once you got the word it was time."

Stipulations that had narrowed the field of possible travel companions considerably. Glad he was not reading anything else into the invitation she had issued him, Hannah relaxed and settled back in her seat. "Ah, the virtues of being an adventure-loving travel writer," she teased.

Joe braked for an armadillo taking his time about crossing the road. As he waited, he grinned at her. "Versus the virtues of being a marketing whiz turned entrepreneur?"

His praise made her flush. Pretending her self-consciousness had nothing to do with him, Hannah wrinkled her nose. "You can't really call me an entrepreneur since the business I'm going to run—*if* I can ever get my dad to retire—has been in the family since Summit was founded in 1847." Since then the mountain town had gone from an isolated but beautiful trading post for ranchers and settlers to a popular getaway and tourist attraction.

The armadillo finally hit the berm. Hands clasping the wheel, Joe drove on. "The changes you want to make are good ones."

He was one of the few people who had seen Hannah's plans to turn around the slowly diminishing family business. Hannah caught a whiff of cinnamon roll as they passed the bakery. "Tell that to my dad."

"I have, a time or two." Joe pressed his lips together ruefully. "Not that he's inclined to listen to an East Coast city slicker like me."

Hannah fidgeted when they stopped at a red light. She was so ready to get to Taipei and begin her new life it was ridiculous. "You grew up in Texas."

"For the first ten years of my life—" Joe waved at a prominent rancher in a pickup truck "—but I went to school in Connecticut."

While she respected Joe's Ivy League credentials, it was the inherently respectful, compassionate way he treated everyone who crossed his path that she admired. Had he intended to stay in the beautiful Trans-Pecos area of West Texas, she might have considered seeing if the two of them could be more than friends.

Unfortunately, she knew it would never happen. He was as much a vagabond at heart as she had once been. For reasons, she suspected, that were just as elusive and privately devastating as her own.

Her mother's death and her father's recent heart attack had made her face the fact that time to address old hurts—or at the very least come to terms with them—was running out. If she wanted to heal the rift between her and her dad, the way her mother had always wanted, it had to be done soon. Whether her dad cooperated or not!

Aware the silence between them had stretched on for too long, Hannah shifted her attention back to Joe and asked casually, "When will you be done with your book?" Last spring, he'd rented a cabin just outside town and used it as a home base for his research on southwest Texas.

"It's essentially done now. I just want to take one more trip to Big Bend, to check out a couple of the hotels I missed on my earlier visits, write the magazine articles I'm going to use to promote the book, and then I'm off to Australia to start my next project."

"So you'll be leaving…?"

"Texas? Right after Labor Day."

Which meant, Hannah thought sadly, she'd rarely if ever see Joe again.

In another three weeks, he'd no longer be stopping by the Mercantile to chat up the tourists shopping there about their favorite haunts in this part of Texas. He'd no longer be teasing her, or making polite conversation with her father. Or stopping by to see if she wanted to grab some lunch at one of the cafés in town, along with whomever else their age he could round up.

Joe turned onto Main Street. The county courthouse and police station sat across from the parklike grounds of the town square, taking one whole block. Farther down, brick buildings some two hundred years old sported colorful awnings over picture windows. In the past few years, restaurants that catered to tourists and natives alike had sprung up here and there, adding to the length of the wide boulevard in the center of town. But it was the imposing Callahan Mercantile & Feed that gave Summit the Old West ambience tourists loved to photograph.

Built shortly after Texas achieved statehood, the sprawling general store still bore the original log-cabin exterior. Improvements had been made over the years, but the wooden rocking chairs scattered across the covered porch that fronted the building still beckoned a person to linger, even after purchases were made.

Joe eased his SUV into a parking space in front of the store. "Any chance the day's pastries have arrived yet?"

Hannah nodded. "My dad stops by the bakery personally every morning to pick them up before he comes in. Help yourself to whatever is there. I'll go find Dad."

Gus was in back, as she figured he would be.

At seventy, he was still a handsome man with expressive brown eyes the same shade as hers. In the two years since her mother's death, his thick straight hair had turned completely white. Gus Callahan had never been an easy man. He was set in his ways. Opinionated. He had a strong sense of right and wrong and had never been known to yield to anyone. Including Hannah.

A lump formed in her throat. Wondering when she would ever stop longing for his approval, she managed to choke out, "Dad?"

He looked up from the account statements he was sorting through.

"I'm leaving," she said wishing, once again, for a miracle.

Gus scowled and set down the stack of billing notices. He looked her square in the eye and said flatly, "It's still not too late to change your mind."

HER TEXAS LAWMAN
by Stella Bagwell

Chief Deputy Ripp McCleod didn't believe the heiress's claim that someone was stalking her. Soon it became clear that Lucita Sanchez was telling the truth and Ripp's interest in the case – and the woman – was growing very personal.

THE PRINCE'S ROYAL DILEMMA
by Brenda Harlen

Innocent Lara can't be Rowan's bride, since she wasn't born in his beautiful Mediterranean principality. The prince faces a tough choice between the country he loves and the woman who has captured his heart…

THE BABY PLAN
by Kate Little

The one thing by-the-book Julia hasn't planned on is pregnancy! Telling Sam that he's going to be a daddy might be a disaster – or it might lead to true love…

FREE!

2 Books
and a surprise gift!

We would like to take this opportunity to thank you for reading this Mills & Boon® book by offering you the chance to take TWO more specially selected titles from the Special Edition series absolutely FREE! We're also making this offer to introduce you to the benefits of the Mills & Boon® Book Club™—

- ★ **FREE home delivery**
- ★ **FREE gifts and competitions**
- ★ **FREE monthly Newsletter**
- ★ **Exclusive Mills & Boon Book Club offers**
- ★ **Books available before they're in the shops**

Accepting these FREE books and gift places you under no obligation to buy, you may cancel at any time, even after receiving your free shipment. Simply complete your details below and return the entire page to the address below. You don't even need a stamp!

YES! Please send me 2 free Special Edition books and a surprise gift. I understand that unless you hear from me, I will receive 4 superb new titles every month for just £3.19 each, postage and packing free. I am under no obligation to purchase any books and may cancel my subscription at any time. The free books and gift will be mine to keep in any case.

E9ZEF

Ms/Mrs/Miss/Mr ....Initials ....
BLOCK CAPITALS PLEASE

Surname ....

Address...

....

....Postcode ....

Send this whole page to:
UK: FREEPOST CN81, Croydon, CR9 3WZ